The Dragon of Lonely Island

REBECCA RUPP

CANDLEWICK PRESS
CAMBRIDGE, MASSACHUSETTS

This is a work of fiction. Names, characters, places,
and incidents are either the product of the author's
imagination or, if real, are used fictitiously.

First paperback edition 2002

The Library of Congress has cataloged the hardcover edition as follows:

Rupp, Rebecca.
The dragon of lonely island / Rebecca Rupp. —1st ed.
p. cm.
Summary: Three children spend the summer with their mother on a
secluded island where they discover a three-headed dragon living in a cave
and learn what it means to be a Dragon Friend.
ISBN 0-7636-0408-9 (hardcover)
[1. Dragon—Fiction. 2. Brothers and sisters—Fiction. 3. Islands—Fiction.]
I. Title.
PZ7.R8886Dr 1998
[Fic]—dc21 97-47759

ISBN 0-7636-1661-3 (paperback)

2 4 6 8 10 9 7 5 3 1

Printed in the United States of America

This book was typeset in Trump Mediaeval.

Candlewick Press
2067 Massachusetts Avenue
Cambridge, Massachusetts 02140

visit us at www.candlewick.com

For Josh and for Ethan,
but most especially for Caleb,
who loves dragons.

Many thanks to all who have helped in the making of this book; among them Amanda, Briana, and Jared Bliss, preliminary readers; Caleb Rupp, who suggested the puzzle box; Ethan Rupp, who repeatedly fixed the computer; Joshua Rupp, who made endless pots of coffee; Joe Spieler and John Thornton, agents and supporters; and very special thanks always to Randy, who makes everything possible, and to Amy Ehrlich, editor, without whose patience, wisdom, and imagination there would be no Fafnyr.

CHAPTER 1

The Island

The summer Hannah was twelve, Zachary ten, and Sarah Emily eight and a half, the Davis children went to stay at their Aunt Mehitabel's house, which stood nearly all by itself on Lonely Island, off the coast of Maine. Aunt Mehitabel did not live in the house. She had an apartment in Philadelphia, which she shared with a miniature bulldog named Henry and an elderly second cousin named Penelope.

Aunt Mehitabel had blue hair, a pince-nez, and a walking stick from Egypt, with an ivory handle carved in the shape of a jackal's head. She was really Father's great-aunt, which made her the children's great-great-aunt.

"To be a great-*great*-aunt, she must be *very* old," said Sarah Emily.

"She must be in her eighties," said Mother, "but it's hard to think of Aunt Mehitabel as old."

Mother had asked Aunt Mehitabel about borrowing the house, because she needed a place where there was peace and quiet to write.

"No telephones," said Mother, "and no neighbors."

Mother wrote mystery novels, and the latest one–*The Secret of Silver House*–had to be finished by September. Mother's novels were published once a year. They all had pictures of girls in long white nightgowns on the covers, running away from castles or through forests or along the edges of rocky cliffs. Hannah, who liked romance, read them at night under her blankets, by flashlight. Zachary, who liked computer games, rockets, and complicated machinery, read *Scientific American* and *Popular Mechanics,* and Sarah Emily, who was shy and overimaginative, read fairy tales.

Sarah Emily was small and pale and wore thick round spectacles with gold rims. Hannah was tall and dark and had naturally curly hair. Zachary was freckled and indeterminate, but Mother said he would look just like Father when he grew up. Father was a marine biologist. He was spending the summer on a ship in the North Atlantic, studying the migratory patterns of *Hyperoodon ampullatus,* the northern bottlenose whale.

Aunt Mehitabel wrote from Philadelphia and sent Mother a set of spare keys to the house. The letter was written in a spidery, old-fashioned script in raspberry pink ink.

"There are caretakers at the house," said Mother, reading from the letter, "named Tobias and Martha Jones. Mr. Jones will take us out to the house in the boat and will fetch our groceries and the mail every day from the mainland. Mrs. Jones will help with the cooking and cleaning." She peered at the children over the top of the page. "Aunt Mehitabel says that Mrs. Jones is not accustomed to children," she said, "so you will have to be on your best behavior."

Hannah made a face.

"Does she say anything else about us?" asked Sarah Emily.

"She sends her love," said Mother, "and says that she's enclosing a special message just for you. It must be in this envelope with your names on it. There's something heavy in it."

The envelope was sealed with green sealing wax.

"What's that?" asked Sarah Emily, pointing.

"Sealing wax. People used to stick letters shut with it a long time ago," said Hannah. "Before they had envelopes with glue on the flap. Sometimes they'd make a print in the sealing wax with a special seal ring to show who the letter was from. Don't you learn anything from all those books you read?"

"Does Aunt Mehitabel have a seal ring?" asked

Sarah Emily. "There's a print in this sealing wax. It's something with a long tail."

"It looks like a lizard," said Zachary. "Pass it over and I'll open it."

Zachary carefully slit the envelope open with his pocketknife, turned it upside down, and shook it gently. A folded slip of paper slid out, and a small iron key with an elaborately curlicued handle. A label was tied to the key. Hannah reached out and turned it over.

"To the Tower Room," she read.

"The tower?" repeated Sarah Emily. "Is Aunt Mehitabel's house a *castle*?"

"Don't be stupid," said Hannah, but Mother put her arm around Sarah Emily and explained that the house was Victorian, built in the 1800s by a sea captain. She showed them a photograph of the house and pointed out the tower. There was a weathervane on top of it in the shape of a clipper ship under full sail. An iron railing ran around the edge of the roof.

"That's called a widow's walk," said Mother. "The women used to stand up there, watching for their husbands to come home from the sea."

"What does the note say?" asked Zachary.

Hannah unfolded the narrow strip of paper. "'If you should find time hanging on your hands,'" she read slowly, "'try exploring Drake's Hill.'"

"What's Drake's Hill?" asked Sarah Emily.

"I have no idea," said Mother, folding the letter back into its envelope. "You'll just have to wait and see. But if Aunt Mehitabel suggests it, it's bound to be something interesting."

Sarah Emily picked up the note and ran a finger over the raspberry pink ink. "Aunt Mehitabel isn't just like everybody else, is she?" she said, but Hannah sighed and made another face.

"I think it all sounds boring," she said. "I don't want to be stuck all summer on some island looking after you two. I'd rather stay here and go rollerblading with Rosalie."

Rosalie was Hannah's best friend. She wore black turtleneck sweaters, took violin and modern-dance lessons, and spent every other weekend in New York City visiting her father and her stepmother. She hardly ever spoke to Zachary or Sarah Emily.

"It will be nice for you to spend some time with your brother and sister," said Mother firmly, "and the island is a beautiful place. You'll see."

Zachary had retreated to the corner of the couch and had buried his head in *Astronomy* magazine. "I think it sounds fun," he said. "There might even be a telescope."

"It's a very old house," said Mother. "There may be all kinds of interesting things."

Sarah Emily repeated dreamily, "Drake's Hill. . . ."

⁂

They arrived at Lonely Island on a glorious day in early July. Mr. Jones met them at the harbor in Chadwick, where they stood on the wharf surrounded by luggage. They had suitcases, knapsacks, and a green canvas duffle bag. There were two sacks of groceries. Sarah Emily wore a backpack. From the unzipped top pocket protruded the fuzzy head of Oberon, the stuffed yellow elephant with one ear who had slept with Sarah Emily since she was two years old. Oberon's single ear flapped in the stiff sea breeze.

Mr. Jones was large, cheerful, and bald. He had a thick gray beard and was wearing a bright orange jacket with a hood. He grinned at Mother and the children and doubtfully eyed the mountain of luggage.

"Miz Davis?"

"And you must be Mr. Jones," Mother said, putting out her hand. Mr. Jones shook it. "And these are my children, Hannah, Zachary, and Sarah Emily."

Mr. Jones shook hands all around. "Very pleased to meet you," he said, "very pleased indeed. It's not often Mrs. Jones and I can look forward to company for the summer."

He gave another glance at the pile of luggage. "This all yours?"

"It certainly is," said Mother.

"The boat's over yonder," said Mr. Jones, pointing

with his chin as he bent down to hoist the two nearest suitcases. "You make yourselves comfortable. I'll load your gear."

They all helped load their belongings onto the boat, which was named the *Martha*–"After Mrs. Jones," Zachary whispered to Sarah Emily–and was painted green. Then they piled into it, Mother and Hannah on the seat in the middle, Zachary and Sarah Emily in the bow.

"Do you know anything about boats?" Mr. Jones asked the children.

"Not much," answered Zachary cautiously. Hannah and Sarah Emily shook their heads.

"Not to worry," said Mr. Jones comfortably, "you will before the summer's over. When you cast off, you unwind the line from this cleat"–he unwound–"and give her a shove." The *Martha,* shoved, bobbled up and down in the water and headed out to sea.

"I could do that," said Zachary.

Mr. Jones chuckled. "Sure you could," he said, "and next time you will."

The boat chugged slowly out of the harbor. The ocean was deep blue, spotted with whitecaps, and a cold salty wind blew the children's hair. Gulls circled and cried overhead. The children huddled in their windbreakers. Hannah, leaning her head against Mother's shoulder, had turned pale. "I wish you'd let me stay home," she said. "This boat is making me sick."

Zachary and Sarah Emily leaned forward, eagerly peering over the waves for the first sight of the island. Suddenly, Sarah Emily gave an excited shout.

"Look!" she cried, pointing. "Is that it?"

Mr. Jones looked pleased. "That's her," he said. "Lonely Island. And that's your house there, dead ahead."

Aunt Mehitabel's house was painted gray, the same color as the rocks on the shore. It was the house of Mother's photograph: There was the tower, topped by the whirling weathervane. Beyond it stood a small cottage, also painted gray, with rows of window boxes planted with bright red geraniums.

"Who lives there?" asked Hannah.

Mr. Jones beamed at her. "I do," he said. "Me and Mrs. Jones and our cat, Buster. We just look after the big place for your auntie."

"Your house is very pretty," said Sarah Emily politely.

The boat pulled up beside a wooden dock, built out from a small rocky beach in a cove below the big house. From the beach, a flight of wooden steps climbed steeply to an iron gate, which opened, squeakily, onto a flagstone path bordered with red-and-black poppies. The path led straight to the house, to the veranda and the front door. The front door was old heavy wood, inset with little panes of stained glass in blue and gold. It was ajar. Mother and the children pushed it open and, followed by Mr. Jones, stepped over the threshold. The house was warm and shining with wax and polish. It smelled deliciously of lemon oil and of cookies baking. Zachary put down his satchel and a bag of groceries and peered into the parlor.

"Look at that!" he said. "There's a stool made out of an elephant's foot!"

"That's horrible," said Hannah, without looking.

Sarah Emily tugged at Zachary's sleeve. "Zachary," she exclaimed, "there's a *telescope!*"

The telescope stood on a tripod next to a towering glass-fronted bookcase filled with old leather-bound books. Zachary gazed at it longingly. "I could track satellites with that," he said. "Or find comets. Or see the Ring Nebula even."

One by one, they tiptoed, fascinated, into Aunt Mehitabel's parlor. The room was vast and dim. The windows were hung with green velvet drapes tied back with tasseled gold cords. Against one wall stood a great Chinese lacquer cabinet with gold trees painted on the doors. There was a brass birdcage, a ship in a bottle, an abacus, and a chess set carved from colored stone.

"Jade?" wondered Zachary.

Mother gazed slowly around the room and then tilted her head back to look up at the high carved ceiling.

She took a deep breath. "My goodness, children," she said. "I never expected anything quite like this."

Mr. Jones poked a cheerful face in the door. "You folks make yourselves at home," he said. "I'll just go let Mrs. Jones know you're here."

"Mr. Jones!" Zachary called. "Who did the telescope belong to?"

"Now, that, I've heard tell, was the captain's own," said Mr. Jones, when Zachary showed it to him. "The captain what built this house a hundred years and more ago."

"Was he a pirate?" Zachary asked hopefully.

Mr. Jones laughed and shook his head. "No more than anyone else in those days," he said, and then, as Zachary's face fell, he added, "but it was a wild life all the same. His ship was called the *Dancing Susan.* That's her on the weathervane up on top of the house."

"Did you *know* the captain?" asked Sarah Emily.

"Of course he didn't," Hannah hissed. "Don't be *stupid.*"

But Mr. Jones just shook his head and chuckled. "He was well before my time, little lady," he said.

Zachary reluctantly turned away from the telescope. "How do you get to the tower?" he asked.

Mr. Jones looked surprised. "The tower? Nobody's been up there in years. It's kept locked."

"Let's explore!" said Sarah Emily, hopping from one foot to the other in excitement. But Mother shook her head at her. "Slow down," she said. "We need to settle in first and then have some supper."

At that moment, the door at the end of the hall flew open and a short plump woman in a calico apron appeared. Her hair was pinned on top of her head in a bun, and there was flour on the end of her nose.

"You must be Mrs. Davis!" she cried, bustling toward them. "And Hannah and Zachary and Sarah Emily! I'm so glad to see you! We've been looking forward to this for weeks! You come along with me and leave Tobias to bring your suitcases up. There's a pot of tea just hot, and fresh lemonade, and raisin cookies just out of the oven."

She wiped her hands on her apron and hustled the children and their mother toward the heavenly smelling kitchen. Zachary, bringing up the rear, tapped Sarah Emily on the shoulder.

"'Not accustomed to children,'" he quoted. "'Be on your best behavior.'"

Sarah Emily giggled. "Even Aunt Mehitabel can't know *everything*," she said.

Chapter 2

The Tower Room

The children's bedrooms were on the second floor of the house, all next to each other in a row, with Zachary at the front of the house, Sarah Emily, who was afraid of the dark, in the middle, and Hannah, who was the oldest and bravest, next to the back staircase. On their first morning at Aunt Mehitabel's house, Sarah Emily woke early. Beside her head, sunbeams danced and flickered across the blue stripes of the wallpaper, and faintly through walls and windows came the rhythmic whoosh and splash of the sea. Sarah Emily stretched out her arms and legs luxuriously in the big four-poster bed. It was a beautiful day and the first real day of vacation. There were a thousand things to do and places to explore. Sarah Emily sprang out of bed, landing on the blue rag rug, and ran next door in her bare feet to wake Zachary.

She paused outside Zachary's door. At home,

Zachary hardly ever let anyone come into his room. He had a sign posted on his door that said NO TRESPASSERS! KEEP OUT!

"I don't like people coming in all the time and fooling around with my things," Zachary said. "I like to be private."

Sarah Emily hesitated for a moment. Then, cautiously, she knocked. "Zachary! Can I come in?"

The door opened. Zachary was awake, already dressed in a T-shirt, blue jeans, and sneakers. Behind him, his bed was made, the quilt pulled smooth, and his pajamas neatly folded on his pillow. Zachary liked everything kept in its proper place. He stepped out into the hall and closed the door firmly behind him. "Is anybody else up?"

"I don't think so," Sarah Emily said. "It's awfully early."

"Then go get dressed," Zachary said. "Let's see what else is in this house. This place is enormous. It must have about a zillion rooms."

"Don't go without me," Sarah Emily said. "I'll be really quick."

When she emerged from her room for the second time, in jeans, sandals, and her favorite pink shirt, Zachary was prowling restlessly up and down the hall.

"This floor is all bedrooms," he whispered.

"There's another big one across the hall next to Mother's and a little one beyond that."

At the very end of the hall a narrow wooden staircase led up and down.

"Where does this go?" asked Sarah Emily. She peered nervously into the shadowy stairwell. "It's spooky in there."

"There's a light," said Zachary reassuringly. He switched it on. "If you go down," he said, "you come out in the kitchen. Mrs. Jones told us so last night. If you go up, I'll bet you get to the attic. Let's go see."

The children tiptoed up the narrow stairs, with Zachary in the lead. The stairs creaked protestingly under their feet.

"Look how dusty these stairs are," Zachary whispered over his shoulder. "Nobody has been up here in ages."

At the top the stairs made an abrupt left-hand turn. The children found themselves facing two closed doors.

"Which one first?" asked Zachary. He deepened his voice in imitation of a magician the children had once seen at a stage show. "Anything could be behind the mysterious doors. A forgotten treasure map. The long-lost family jewels."

Sarah Emily giggled. "A magic carpet, all rolled up in a corner. A crystal ball."

"Or a skeleton," Zachary said. "Or ghosts!"

Sarah Emily shivered. "Don't, Zachary. You're scaring me."

Zachary closed his eyes and pointed dramatically. "I pick . . . the door on the left!"

Sarah Emily tugged nervously at his sleeve. "Maybe we should wait for Hannah."

"We can show her everything later," Zachary said. "Aren't you curious? Let's just take a quick look." He turned the wooden doorknob and pulled open the door. "Come on, S. E. Not a ghost in sight."

Before them was a long dim room, stacked floor to ceiling with odds and ends. There was a torn green velvet sofa with feet shaped like crocodile claws, stacks of crumbling magazines tied up with twine, old leather trunks, a wire dressmaker's dummy, and an aged upright piano with three missing keys.

"Look at all this stuff," said Sarah Emily, awed.

"This is *great,*" said Zachary enthusiastically. "Look up there–I think that's a *sword.* We'll have to come back. Let's go see what's behind the other door. Maybe this place has *two* attics. It's big enough."

But the other door was locked. Zachary rattled the doorknob and shoved the wooden panels–"Maybe it's just stuck," said Sarah Emily hopefully–but the door refused to budge.

"It's locked," said Zachary finally. "We can't get in."

"Maybe the Joneses have the key," suggested Sarah Emily. "We could ask."

Zachary's eyes suddenly opened wide. "Wait a minute," he said. "Don't move, S. E. I'll be right back." He turned and raced down the stairs. In less than a minute, he was back, clutching something in his hand. He grinned triumphantly at Sarah Emily as he opened his fingers. There in his outstretched hand lay Aunt Mehitabel's little iron key, with its curiously curlicued handle and attached paper tag. "We *have* a key," he said.

Sarah Emily's eyes widened too. "Do you suppose . . . ," she began.

Zachary nodded. "This must be the Tower Room."

The key fit. It slid precisely into the lock and turned with a sharp click. Zachary tried the knob once more and this time the door, released, opened. In front of them was an iron ladder leading up to a trap door in the boards of the floor overhead.

"It *is* the Tower Room," breathed Sarah Emily.

"Come on," said Zachary. "I'll go first. Let's climb."

Rung by rung, they mounted the iron ladder. Zachary pushed on the trap door–"It's heavy," he panted–and slowly thrust it open. It tilted back on its hinges and the children scrambled out onto the floor. They got to their feet and slowly looked around. "Wow!" Zachary said.

The children stood in a small octagonal room, completely circled by round windows that looked like portholes. They could see the entire island from the windows of the tower. To the north, at the far end of the island, a rocky hill rose up, topped with windblown trees.

"I'll bet that's Drake's Hill," Zachary said.

Sarah Emily turned away from the window.

"This was a kid's room once," she said. "A playroom. Look–the toys are still here."

"Maybe it was Aunt Mehitabel's," Zachary said, "when she was little."

On shelves along one wall, beneath the round windows, were rows of books and old-fashioned toys: a wooden doll with glossy painted hair, a jar of colored marbles, a folded checkerboard, a small blue china tea set with a chipped teapot. There was a collection of shells and chunks of coral. Two immense pink conch shells, too large for the shelves, were set on the floor below. There was a brass gong on a stand, with a little red wooden hammer hanging on a hook at its side. Sarah Emily gently unhooked the hammer and tapped the gong. It gave off a mellow bell-like chime.

"Look at this," said Zachary from the other side of the room. "Wouldn't you love to have a desk like this?" The desk closed with a wooden flap, fastened with a small metal hook. Opened, the flap folded down to form a flat writing surface. The back of the desk was lined with rows and rows of little cubbyholes–"They're called pigeonholes," Zachary said–filled with papers, packets, boxes, and jars. There was a neat row of bottles of colored inks.

"I didn't know ink came in so many different colors," said Sarah Emily. She began reading the labels on the little bottles one by one. "Lilac. Magenta. Emerald Green. Topaz. Aquamarine. Gold."

Zachary was busily opening and closing the desk drawers.

"Nothing special here," he said. "Just paper and envelopes and stuff. Let me try the big drawer at the bottom."

The drawer smoothly slid open.

"It's on little wheels," Zachary said.

"What's in it?" asked Sarah Emily.

The drawer was empty, except for a wooden box. Zachary lifted out the box and set it on the desktop. It was about the size of an ordinary shoebox, but much heavier, made out of dark polished wood. The top of the box was inlaid with a pattern of interlocking squares and rectangles, made of pieces of wood in different colors, from pale gold to chocolate brown to ebony. Sarah Emily ran her fingers slowly from piece to piece, tracing the patterns. "It's beautiful," she said. "How do you open it?"

The box had no visible handle or latch, and it was sealed tightly shut. The children poked, prodded, and wiggled the box, turned it sideways and upside down, and–Zachary was frustrated–even shook it. But nothing happened. There seemed to be no way of opening it. Then, as they stared at each other, undecided about what to do next, they heard a faint voice calling their names from far below.

"Zachary! Sarah Emily! Where are you? It's time for breakfast!"

"That's Mother," said Sarah Emily. "We'd better go."

Zachary set the box back in the bottom desk drawer. "We'll figure it out," he said. "We'll come back later."

"Zachary!" Mother called again. "Sarah Emily!"

Hastily the children climbed through the trap door and scrambled down the iron ladder. Zachary closed the door to the Tower Room, locked it, and carefully put the key back in his pocket.

"I'm starving," said Sarah Emily. "It feels like we've been up there for hours."

"We're right here!" Zachary shouted. "We're coming!"

They hurried down the stairs toward the tempting smell of frying bacon.

CHAPTER 3

Fafnyr Goldenwings

The children sat on the veranda steps eating home-made doughnuts sprinkled with powdered sugar, made just that morning by Mrs. Jones.

"This is the most wonderful place on earth," said Sarah Emily blissfully, licking her fingers.

They sat for a few minutes in stuffed silence. Bumblebees buzzed happily in the red rosebushes along the garden fence, and on the shore the waves rolled in and out, crashing against the rocks. From somewhere inside the house came the sound of Mrs. Jones singing "Amazing Grace" slightly off-key. Sarah Emily shaded her eyes with her hand and peered northward. There, small in the distance, the rocky hill topped with windblown trees was silhouetted against the sky.

"Drake's Hill," she said.

Zachary nodded. "It *is* Drake's Hill," he said. "I

asked Mr. Jones. He said that's what Aunt Mehitabel always called it."

"When do we go explore it?" Sarah Emily pursued. "Like Aunt Mehitabel said in her note."

Zachary jumped to his feet. "Right now," he said. "As soon as we can get ready. It's too nice a day to stay inside. It's probably farther to that hill than it looks, though. We should take some provisions."

"Doughnuts," said Sarah Emily immediately.

"Water," said Zachary practically. "Sweaters, in case it gets cold. Band-Aids. A compass, maybe."

"We'd better tell Hannah," said Sarah Emily. "Maybe she'll want to go too."

Hannah was in her bedroom with the door closed.

"Hannah doesn't like anything anymore," Sarah Emily had said to Mother when Hannah first started closing her door. "All she likes is that old Rosalie. And she's always saying that I'm stupid."

"You're not stupid," Mother had said, "and Hannah still loves you. She's just growing up and that's harder than it looks. Be patient."

Now Sarah Emily patiently tapped on Hannah's door and–when Hannah shouted, "What is it?"–explained the plan to explore Drake's Hill. Hannah decided that she might as well go along. "I guess there's nothing better to do," Hannah said ungraciously, strapping on her sandals.

They told Mother where they were going. "That's fine, darlings," Mother said. "Don't be gone too long–and, Hannah, take care of your younger brother and sister. I count on you to make sure no one gets hurt or does anything foolish."

Mrs. Jones told them that it was about an hour's walk to the hill. "There used to be a path there, but Mr. Jones and I don't go up that way these days; my knees aren't up to it," Mrs. Jones said. "You'll need a snack to eat along the way." Within the hour, the three children were ready to set out, carrying a picnic lunch–sandwiches, apples, raisin cookies, and a bottle of lemonade–in Zachary's backpack. The pack also held a compass, a flashlight, Zachary's Swiss Army knife (with six knife blades, a screwdriver, a corkscrew, and a tiny toothpick), a notebook and pencil, and–Hannah worried about her complexion–a bottle of sunscreen.

The day grew hotter as the sun rose higher, though the sea wind was cool. Gulls cried high in the sky, and in the grass beneath their feet, green grasshoppers leaped with a whirring of wings. The children headed straight for the hill. As they walked, a faint, worn track became visible. "There *is* a path," said Sarah Emily.

"Heading right where we want to go," said Zachary. "Let's follow it."

They strode along, single file because the old path was so narrow. Sarah Emily hummed as she walked. Zachary paused every once in a while to check directions on his compass. Hannah dabbed sunscreen on her nose. Soon Zachary and Sarah Emily were hungry again–"I can't believe you two, after eating all those doughnuts," said Hannah–so they paused, just at the foot of the hill, for a sandwich (peanut butter and Mrs. Jones's homemade strawberry jam), a cookie, and a drink of lemonade. Zachary's freckles began to come out in the sun. Sarah Emily crumpled the last sandwich wrapper and tucked it back into Zachary's pack. "Let's go to the very top," she said, "and look for China."

"Wrong direction and wrong ocean," said Hannah. "Try France."

"Or Greenland," said Zachary. "Last one to the top is a rotten egg!" He grabbed the pack and began to run, bounding up the little path, winding in and out around scattered boulders.

Hannah and Sarah Emily–shouting "Hey!" and "Wait for me!"–dashed after him.

The hill was steeper than it looked. Soon the children were breathless, and one after another they slowed, panting, to a walk. They were hot, and the backs of Sarah Emily's legs began to ache. They staggered up the last few feet and collapsed, laughing, against the huge heap of piled rocks that formed the very peak of Drake's Hill. Zachary raised his fist in triumph. "Excelsior!" he shouted.

The view from the hill was spectacular. From their height, they could trace the coast of the island and gaze far out to sea. "I feel like I've just climbed Mount Everest," said Hannah.

"Let's get right up on top of these rocks," said Zachary. "Then we'll be able to see everything in both directions."

They scrambled up the side of the great heap of gray boulders, scrabbling for footholds as they climbed. The rocks were piled like giant jumbled steps. There were short heaving climbs–Sarah Emily, whose legs were short, needed to be boosted by Zachary and Hannah–then expanses of level flatness, then more steep climbs. At the last flat step, as they approached the peak, they came to a smooth, sheer wall, higher than Hannah's head, with not so much as a crack or a crevice in sight. "Let's go back," said Sarah Emily. "It's too high."

But Zachary refused to give up.

"Maybe we can get up from the other side," he said.

The step–more like a rocky shelf–curved around to the right, almost like a walkway circling the very top of the hill. The children cautiously edged their way around it. Sarah Emily, who hated heights, refused to look down. On the north side of the rock face, the shelf suddenly widened out into a broad platform, high above and overlooking the empty sea.

"Look at *that*!" gasped Sarah Emily.

"A cave!" said Zachary.

At the back of the stone platform, a wide gaping opening led back into darkness.

"Let's go inside," said Zachary eagerly, but Sarah Emily hung back.

"Let's not," she said. "There could be anything in there. Bears or something. And besides, it smells funny."

Zachary and Hannah sniffed the air. Near the cave entrance, there was a strange odor: the smell of charcoal and smoke, with a hint of something tangier, spicy, alien.

"Probably just old campfires," said Zachary. "Maybe Mr. and Mrs. Jones used to come up here and roast marshmallows." He peered blindly into the darkness, then turned to fumble in his backpack. "Just a minute," he said. "I brought my flashlight."

He switched it on and cautiously stepped forward into the cave. Sarah Emily and Hannah crowded behind him. The three children, clinging to each other, edged slowly inward. As they moved into the cave, the sound of the sea abruptly shut off, as though someone had thrown a massive switch. The cave floor seemed to slant downward into the hill, and inside, it felt enormous; there was a sense of soaring subterranean spaces. Zachary's flashlight barely penetrated the gloom. "It didn't look this big from the outside," Sarah Emily whispered. Groping, they stretched out their arms, left and right, to the sides.

"Can anybody feel a wall anywhere?" Zachary asked softly. Nobody could.

"This place is simply huge," said Hannah. "The whole inside of the hill must be hollow."

"It feels endless," said Sarah Emily nervously.

The children shuffled forward, feeling gingerly with their feet. "There could be deep holes," said Sarah Emily. The strange sharp smell–smoke? sulfur?–got stronger.

"You know what I wonder?" said Zachary. "Where did this hill get its name anyway? Was the sea captain who built the house named Drake? How come it's called Drake's Hill?"

There was a sudden shifting sound from the back of the cave, a heavy sandpapery scraping noise. Then there came a soft hiss in the darkness–the sound of a lighted blowtorch, thought Zachary–and a red-and-yellow flare of flame. The interior of the cave leaped into light. Before the children's astonished eyes, a vast expanse of gold flashed and glittered. There before them lay a long reptilian body, curled comfortably on the cave floor, with a coiled golden tail, ending in a flat arrowhead-shaped point. Two eyes–sharp slits of jade green–glared at them out of the darkness.

"It is called Drake's Hill, young man," said a deep, raspy voice, "because *drake* is an ancient and honorable name for *dragon.* The hill is named after *me.*"

The children clutched each other–so hard, Hannah said later, that her arm turned black and blue–and gaped unbelievingly at the dragon.

"A . . . *dragon*?" said Zachary, in a high, unfamiliar voice. Hannah could feel her knees trembling. Sarah Emily burst into tears.

There was a frozen pause. The dragon extended its golden neck to its greatest length and peered intently at the three children, down the length of its golden nose. It seemed to be studying a trio of particularly unpromising scientific specimens.

Suddenly, Hannah squared her shoulders, put her arm around Sarah Emily, and stepped forward.

"You're scaring my little sister," she said.

The dragon drew back and its voice softened.

"My dear young lady," it said apologetically, "I never dreamed. . . . Nothing could be further from my intentions. . . ."

The golden head swiveled toward Sarah Emily.

"Despite my intimidating form," it said, "I am

quite peaceful. Consistently kindhearted. Almost invariably harmless."

"It's all right," said Hannah. She gave Sarah Emily a squeeze. "He's gentle. He won't hurt you."

"Please," said the dragon, "don't cry. I can't bear to hear children cry."

Sarah Emily sniffled and rubbed the back of her hand across her eyes.

"In all the fairy tales," she said in a tearful voice, "dragons are always burning down villages. And kidnapping princesses and eating them."

The dragon gave a sarcastic snort.

"Ridiculous," it said. "*Princesses!*" It repeated the word with loathing. "No self-respecting dragon . . . ," it began. Then it seemed to change its mind. The golden head drooped sadly. "Clearly," the dragon said in a mournful voice, "I have been forgotten. Dragons used to be quite well known in your world, respectfully looked up to. Admired, even." There was a resigned pause. "Of course, that was a long time ago. And your kind is ephemeral. One cannot expect of humans the prodigious memory exhibited by dragonkind."

"I don't understand," said Sarah Emily. And then, in a whisper to Hannah, "What is he talking about?"

"Ephemeral means short-lived," Hannah whispered back. "He's saying that human beings don't last very long. And prodigious means big. He means that dragons remember a lot better than we do."

The dragon nodded. "Precisely," it said. It seemed to reflect for a moment. "What year is it?" it finally asked.

The children told it, and the dragon frowned in thought, then scratched something with its claw on the cave floor. "Borrow from the nine," it muttered. "Or was it carry four?" It studied its work a moment, then frustratedly crossed the scratchings out. "One hundred and seventeen years," it said impressively. "I have been asleep for one hundred and seventeen years." There was a brief pause. Then the dragon said, in less exalted tones, "Or maybe seventy-one. I was never very good at mathematics."

"Do dragons always sleep that long?" asked Zachary.

The dragon gave him another long look down its golden nose. "There is no *always* about dragons, my dear boy. I cannot speak for my brother and sister here; they have been awake in more recent times. But I like my rest."

"Brother and sister?" asked Hannah.

The dragon nodded. "*We,*" it said proudly, "are a tridrake."

The children looked puzzled. "*What?*" whispered Sarah Emily.

"A tridrake," the dragon repeated. "A three-headed dragon."

Only then did the children notice that the dragon had two other necks, branching off on either side of the first neck, and two other heads, nestled on either shoulder, both with eyes closed, sound asleep.

"Our name," said the dragon, pulling itself to a sitting position and wriggling into an upright and elegant pose, "is Fafnyr Goldenwings."

"I'm Hannah," said Hannah. "Hannah Davis. And these are my brother and sister, Zachary and Sarah Emily."

Fafnyr nodded majestically at each child.

"Hannah. Zachary. Sarah Emily. Two daughters"—the dragon studied the girls and then turned its head toward Zachary—"and one son. And you, dear boy, are the eldest?"

"No," said Zachary. "I'm ten. Hannah is the oldest."

The dragon looked at Hannah with a sympathetic eye. "There are many trials involved in being the oldest," it said. "I, myself, of the three Heads, was the First Awake. It is a great responsibility to lead the way."

"First Awake?" repeated Hannah, puzzled.

Sarah Emily echoed her. "What does First Awake mean?"

"When a young tridrake is ready to hatch out of the

egg," the dragon explained, "one Head wakes first, cracks open the eggshell, and emerges into the open air. This Head, the First Awake, is the eldest of the three–in this case, of course, myself. The second Head wakes next, and finally the third. The third–the Last Awake–is the youngest of the Heads."

Zachary nudged Sarah Emily. "That would be you, S.E.," he said. "Of the three of us, you're the Last Awake."

Sarah Emily still looked confused. "I think it would be awfully muddling," she said. "To have three different heads, I mean. Can you tell the other heads what to do? Are you all one dragon or are you three different dragons?"

"Yes," the dragon said. Then it shook its head. "No. It's a little difficult to explain." It closed its eyes for a moment and breathed deeply through its nose. "Each Head is its own dragon, though we all share the same–quite attractive, don't you think?–body." The dragon rearranged its tail and flexed its golden wings. "Still, though each Head is different, we share the same memories, the same experiences. . . ."

It paused. Then it said, "They know what I know and I know what they know. If you see what I mean."

"I think so," said Hannah.

Sarah Emily nodded.

"So," said Zachary, "when the other heads wake

up, they'll both know all about us? About Hannah and Sarah Emily and me?"

"Precisely," the dragon said. "It will be as though they had been with us too."

Hannah had another question. "Fafnyr," she asked, "why are you here? On this island?"

The great golden dragon slowly closed its gleaming green eyes and opened them again. "This, my dear, is a Resting Place. A safe haven." It sighed deeply and studied its claws. "There are fewer and fewer such Places left these days. You humans are an uncommonly intrusive lot."

"*What?*" whispered Sarah Emily.

"People are nosy," Zachary whispered back. "They're always snooping around, exploring things."

"The world is not always a congenial place for dragons," the dragon continued, in put-upon tones. "We have been worshipped and admired. We have been–quite foolishly–feared. And we have been pursued and persecuted. At times we have found it wise to withdraw from public society."

The dragon paused.

Then it said confidingly, "We also need to take naps."

"Who would persecute a dragon?" Sarah Emily asked. "Think how big they are. They have huge claws. And they breathe fire."

"Well," said Hannah, "in the Middle Ages, the knights were always riding out to slay dragons."

"That was because of the princesses," began Zachary. "Dragons were always kidnapping . . ."

The dragon gave him a scathing look. "Young man," it interrupted, "that is precisely the problem. Rumor. Gossip. Slander. You humans are so often hostile to the unusual, so ready to believe the worst."

The dragon raised its right front claws as though it were taking an oath.

"Dragons," it said firmly, "do *not* capture princesses. They could, of course, princesses being the feather-brained creatures that they are, but they don't. What would be the point? A princess, once you've got it, is a poor conversationalist. It whines and complains. It refuses to sit down on the rocks for fear of muddying its gown."

"But if you never capture princesses," Sarah Emily said, in an apprehensive voice, "then what do you eat?"

The dragon gave the children a withering stare.

"I see," it said, "that you share some common misconceptions about dragons. We are, as a species, vegetarian." It cleared its throat. "Well, largely vegetarian. A green salad, a few bushels of fruit, whole-wheat grain products." It lowered its voice and added, somewhat indistinctly, "An occasional fish."

"We didn't know that," said Hannah.

"Of course not," said the dragon. "And so few humans bother to ask. Most simply *assume.*"

"But not all?" asked Hannah.

The dragon turned its head toward Hannah and again the jade green eyes softened.

"No," the dragon said, "not all. That reminds me of a story–a tale of a human who understood dragons. She too was a First Awake. An eldest daughter. Like you, my dear."

The dragon gave a little sigh and its green eyes seemed to glisten. "It happened very long ago," the dragon said, "and in another place, far away. Long ago," it repeated sorrowfully, "and far away."

The dragon was still for a moment. Then it ruffled up its golden wings and settled itself more comfortably. "Sit down," the dragon said, "and listen."

Sarah Emily lay down on her stomach on the cave's stone floor and rested her chin on her hands, the way she did when she listened to Mother's bedtime stories. The stone was beautifully warm, softly heated by the dragon's inner fire. Zachary and Hannah leaned back against Fafnyr's smooth golden tail. They lost themselves in the pictures brought into their minds by Fafnyr's voice. It seemed, as the dragon spoke, that the walls of the cave dissolved. There was a sudden green scent of fresh plants and newly plowed soil, a chatter of foreign voices, bird song, and the soft distant gong of a temple bell. A warm wind lifted their hair. Suddenly they were inside the dragon's story, seeing the world through someone else's eyes.

The Green-Eyed Dragon's Story

Chapter 4

Mei-lan

"Long, long ago, in the land called China," the dragon said, "in the days before the emperor ordered the building of the Great Wall, a young girl named Mei-lan lived with her family in a tiny village in the foothills of the mountains. . . .

It was a green and pleasant place filled with brooks and fruit trees, and Mei-lan's father, who had a little farm, did well. The rains came and the crops were good and the villagers were happy. But some were happier than others. In those days in China, daughters were considered worthless, and Mei-lan, whose two younger brothers were much more important than she was, seemed to be the most worthless of all. The interests of the family's two sons–Plum Boy and Little Peach–always came first. If there were not enough sweets to go around, Mei-lan always had to go without. If Mei-lan had something that the boys wanted–a favorite toy, a brightly-colored bird's feather, or a sparkly stone–she had to give it up. When the nights became cold, Mei-lan always had to sleep the farthest from the burning stove so that the boys could stay warm. This, as far as Mei-lan knew, was the way things had always been and the way things always would be. But sometimes it was hard and it made her unhappy. So it went on, until one day, when she went to the mountainside to gather firewood. . . .

Mei-lan knew she shouldn't be angry–Plum Boy and Little Peach were boys, after all, and their wishes were much more important than those of a lowly girl–but sometimes life was hard to bear. Just that morning, Plum Boy, who was six years old, had demanded Mei-lan's pet, a shiny brown cricket named Moon Singer, who Mei-lan kept in a tiny bamboo cage next to her sleeping mat. Mei-lan had captured Moon Singer in a field near the river and brought him home. He was a friendly little soul, cheerful and bright eyed, whose comforting creak and chirp helped lull her to sleep each night. She fed him bits of green leaves and lotus seeds and he seemed to recognize her voice, climbing on her finger when she called him and brushing his long antennae against her cheek when she lifted him up to her face.

When Plum Boy took Moon Singer for his own, Mei-lan felt as though her heart would break. "Please, Honorable Brother, accept this unworthy gift," she had said, but her voice trembled, and when Plum Boy gleefully carried the cricket away, she couldn't hold back her tears. Now, alone on the mountainside collecting kindling for the family cooking fire, she thought dismally about Moon Singer. "I will never have another pet," Mei-lan told herself bitterly. "If I have nothing, nothing can be taken away from me." She was starting to cry again, wiping away the tears with the sleeve of her pink quilted jacket, when a sound in the thicket behind her made her stop sniffling and listen. There it came again: a scraping rattle and a muffled moan that sounded like a creature in pain.

Forgetting her own sorrows, Mei-lan ran to investigate. She pushed and shoved her way through the tangled underbrush, pulling aside branches and pausing to untangle the brambles that were caught in her clothes and her hair. Suddenly she burst out of the thicket into a small clearing, in the middle of which lay . . .

Mei-lan dropped on her knees and her mouth fell open in amazement. "An Honorable Dragon," she breathed.

The dragon lay on its side, its head resting in the grass and its jade green eyes dim and clouded with pain. Two other heads, Mei-lan saw, were snuggled down, motionless on its shoulders, eyes closed, seemingly fast asleep. One great golden wing was torn and bloodied and bent over its back at a strange and painful-looking angle. The dragon looked despairingly at Mei-lan, took one long shuddering breath, moaned again, and lay still. All thoughts of her own problems vanished from Mei-lan's mind. She ran forward and took the golden dragon's head in her arms. The glittering scales felt hot and dry to her touch and the dragon simply leaned, limp and heavy, against her. "Oh, Honorable Dragon," Mei-lan cried in panic, "please don't die!"

The dragon struggled for a moment and managed to speak. "An archer," it said weakly. "An ambush." It gestured toward its left shoulder and Mei-lan saw the shaft of an arrow thrust through the golden scales and deep into the dragon's flesh. Mei-lan gave a gasp of horror.

"He shot me," the dragon said, "and I fell." It closed its eyes exhaustedly for a moment, then opened them again and looked sorrowfully at Mei-lan. "He did not know who I was."

Mei-lan bowed her head. "It has been a very long time since the Great Ones have been seen in this land. Perhaps some ignorant persons have forgotten."

The dragon sighed deeply. "I am hurt," it said, and lay its head down again.

Mei-lan knew that something must be done immediately if the dragon were to survive. She laid a small cool hand on the dragon's golden head. "I will be back soon," she promised. She moved gently away from the dragon, so as not to jar the broken wing, and then ran, forcing her way through the thicket, hurling herself pell-mell down the mountainside.

"Mother! Father!" she shouted, as she burst through the gate at home. "An Honorable Dragon on the mountainside! A dragon! He needs help! Oh, please, please, come quickly!"

Mother, in a jacket patterned with crimson peonies, was preparing tea. Father was eating rice balls. As Mei-lan flung herself into the room, Mother straightened up and Father laid down his chopsticks. "Mei-lan," Mother said reprovingly, "it is not respectful to greet your parents in this rowdy fashion."

Father shook his head. "We will never find you a husband," he said.

Mei-lan forced herself to become calm. "I'm sorry," she said. "I'm sorry, Mother. I am sorry, Father. But there is an Honorable Dragon–a Great One–on the mountainside and he is injured. He needs our help. Please, I don't know what to do. Should we send for the villagers? The mayor and the doctor? What should we do?"

Her parents stared at her in disbelief. "Mei-lan, this tale cannot be true," said Mother.

"But he spoke to me!" Mei-lan cried. "He said, 'I am hurt!' He will die *if we don't help him!"*

Father frowned. "No Great One," he pronounced, "would speak to a worthless girl-child. The Great Ones once were known to speak to emperors and scholars, high-born men of great wisdom and learning. But never, not even before the days of my great-grandfather's grandfather, when the Great Ones were seen more often in this land, would an Honorable Dragon have stooped to speak with such as you."

"Perhaps not," said Mei-lan humbly, bowing her head, "but this dragon had no choice. He is hurt. He was wounded by an arrow and he fell. I think his wing is broken. He needs our help."

Father shook his head. "You must cease to discuss this dragon, Mei-lan. This cannot be. You imagined it."

"I did *not* imagine it!" cried Mei-lan, stamping her foot in frustration. "The dragon is real and he is on our mountainside right now!"

"Mei-lan!" said Father sternly. "You must learn to control your temper."

"Perhaps the child is ill," said Mother, worriedly. "Perhaps we should take her to the doctor."

The doctor lived in one of the biggest houses in the village. It had a red-painted gate, and a courtyard planted with flowering trees, and a stone pool filled with goldfish. The doctor had *a long drooping mustache and wore a yellow silk robe with a matching yellow silk cap. He listened gravely as Mei-lan's father explained the problem and then solemnly felt Mei-lan's forehead to see if she had a fever. He slowly shook his head.*

"The girl has had a touch of the sun," he said. And then, turning to Mei-lan, he explained kindly, "It is easy when one is hot and tired to imagine that sun glinting off pale branches looks like gold. Your dragon is all in your mind. Some scholars say that dragons were merely inventions of the mind, stories made up long ago by poets and songwriters. You did not see a dragon, because there was no dragon there." He shook his head again, sat down in his lacquered chair, and picked up a book. "There are no dragons," he repeated. Mei-lan's father bowed and apologized for disturbing him and took Mei-lan away.

In the street on the way home, they met the village mayor, a tall and imposing man wearing a coat embroidered with lilies and kingfishers. He carried a tiny dog in his wide sleeve. The mayor and Mei-lan's father bowed and exchanged greetings. "You have been visiting the Honorable Doctor?" the Mayor asked. "I hope none of your worthy family is ill."

"No, we are well. But this foolish one," Mei-lan's father said, gesturing toward Mei-lan, "this ignorant girl, claims to have seen a dragon on the mountainside."

"A dragon?" The Mayor laughed, and the little dog in his sleeve jiggled up and down. "Ridiculous. There are no dragons. They all died long ago. And even if one were still alive, no Great One would speak to a simple girl. The child is lying."

"Of course, Honorable One," said Father respectfully, bowing to the mayor. Then, as the mayor pompously paraded on down the street, Father turned to his daughter and said sharply, "Come, Mei-lan, we must return home."

"There will be no more talk of this dragon," Father said, as they passed through their own gate and entered the house. "You will apologize to me and to your Honorable Mother, and you will cease to make up these unfortunate stories. You have embarrassed all of us. You have been most upsetting."

Mei-lan gave up. "I understand, Father,"

she said. "I apologize. I have made a stupid mistake. I will go back and fetch the firewood now." She bowed politely to her parents and left the room. But as soon as her feet, in their little straw sandals, crossed the threshold, she began to run, an expression of obstinate determination on her face. From the shelf in the big front room, she snatched up her sleeping quilt, folded it small, and rolled it into a tight bundle. From the storage cupboard in the corner, she took a bolt of cotton cloth–"Bandages," she thought–and a pot of the green herbal medicine that her grandmother claimed would cure anything, from snakebite to broken bones. She stuffed a handful of sugared rice cakes into a carrying pouch, and paused at the farmyard well to fill a wooden bucket with cold water. Then, staggering under her load, she headed back, as fast as she could, to the mountainside.

The dragon was still there. It looked paler and its golden scales were dull. Its jade green eyes were closed, but at the sound of Mei-lan pushing her way through the thicket, it opened them and gazed at her helplessly. Mei-lan knelt and stroked its golden head. "It will be all right, Honorable One," she said, though secretly she was far from sure that this was true. "I will help you." Gently she raised the dragon's head so that it could have a cool drink from the bucket. The dragon lapped gratefully and gave a sigh of relief. Then she fed it the rice cakes, one by one. Then another drink of water.

"Better," the dragon said faintly. "It is better now. Thank you, Small Daughter."

"Honorable Dragon," Mei-lan said, "I could not get help for you. The doctor says that dragons never existed. The mayor says that all dragons died long ago. And no one, not even my Honorable Parents, believes that a Great One would speak to a mere girl. There is no one to treat your wounds or to speak to you with words of wisdom. There is only me. But I will do the best I can."

The dragon's eyes flared briefly, a brighter, sharper green.

"They have all *forgotten me?" it said incredulously.*

"It has been a very long time," Mei-lan said gently, "since you have shown yourself. In our village, no dragon has been seen before, not in my father's time, or my grandfather's, or even in the days of my grandfather's grandfather. If

our people had seen you, they would remember. No one could possibly forget you.*"*

There was a pause.

"Perhaps," Mei-lan went on in a smaller voice, "if someone else had found you . . . someone important . . . "

But the dragon had closed its eyes again.

Mei-lan lifted her chin determinedly and cleared her throat. "If you can roll over on your side," she said, "I will try to treat your wounds." The dragon rolled over so that Mei-lan could reach the injured wing. Carefully she bathed the cuts and tears with a pad of cloth, wiping away the dried blood and dirt. She grasped the shaft of the arrow and, wincing, pulled it out of the dragon's shoulder. Angrily she flung the arrow to the ground. Then, gritting her teeth, she seized the huge golden wing with both hands and pulled it back into position. There was a sharp clicking sound as the wing snapped back into place. It looked normal now and folded neatly across the dragon's back, just as it was supposed to do. She smeared the arrow wound with the herbal salve and–tearing the cotton cloth into long strips–wrapped it in clean bandages.

The dragon settled itself more comfortably

in the grass. "The pain is going," it said. "Thank you, child. You have done well. I think I shall go to sleep now." The green eyes closed for a moment, then flickered open. "Sing to me," the dragon said sleepily.

So Mei-lan sat and stroked the dragon's head and sang to it, a peaceful, sleepy song about crickets and moonbeams and white incense-smelling flowers that open only on starry nights. And soon the dragon slept. Mei-lan covered as much of it as she could with her sleeping quilt and silently tiptoed away.

CHAPTER 5

The Barbarians from the North

Every day Mei-lan returned to the mountain to care for the dragon. She brought it tea and rice, and ginger-flavored soup with pork and bamboo shoots, and more green salve for its wound. One afternoon she even hauled buckets of hot soapy water up the slope to the thicket and gave the dragon a bath. Its golden scales began to gleam and sparkle again. While the dragon was healing, she sang it songs and told it stories, and–since the dragon was a good listener–she told it about her life at home and how hard it was to be thought of as a worthless girl. She told it about the loss of her pet cricket, Moon Singer. Telling the dragon all these troubles didn't change things, but it made her feel better. Just talking to the dragon gave her a feeling of strength and peace.

Then one day, as she came down from the mountainside, she found the village in an uproar. News had come from the North. The messenger even now was sitting on a bench in the town square, mopping his face with a handkerchief and drinking a glass of rice wine. Everyone seemed to be talking at once and faces were fearful. Some of the women and the smallest children were in tears. "The Mongols!" Mei-lan heard over and over again. "The Mongol horsemen are invading!" "The Mongols are upon us!"

Mei-lan felt a pang of terror. Ever since she was very small, she had been told frightening stories about the Mongol horsemen–the fierce barbarian tribes from the North who killed and burned everything in their path. In some stories, they rode monstrous black horses with flaming red nostrils and eyes and carried battle-axes, swords, and spears. The villages they passed through were left smoking ruins, with not so much as a cat or dog still alive. People said "The barbarians are coming!" as a joke when any small disaster or trouble approached. Father even said it at the annual arrival of the tax collector. But a real invasion of the vicious warriors was a terror beyond imagining. There were no jokes in the village now.

At home, Mei-lan found her parents frantically packing, preparing to flee into the hills. The family's few valuables–a bag of coins, six silver spoons, the jeweled pin shaped like a butterfly that Mother wore in her hair on special occasions–were hastily wrapped in a quilt. Father was tying together a bundle of tools. Plum Boy–clutching the precious cage containing Moon Singer–and Little Peach–wide-eyed with fright–were sitting on the floor next to a sack stuffed with clothing.

"Go pack some food for our journey, Mei-lan," Mother snapped as she rushed frenziedly about the house. "Rice and meat. A bottle of green tea. Anything you can find." Mei-lan

turned obediently toward the kitchen, where fresh rice steamed in the family cooking pot–and then, with a quick glance behind her, slipped out the door and began to run toward the mountain, faster than she had ever run before.

The dragon was awake and watching for her as she crashed through the thicket and collapsed at its feet, gasping for breath. For a few moments she was unable to speak. The dragon was concerned.

"Child, what is wrong?" it asked. "What has happened?"

Mei-lan hid her face in her hands. "The barbarians are coming! The Mongols from the North! They will kill us all and burn our village! Oh, please, please, most Honorable Dragon, can't you help us?"

The dragon frowned. "I have little love for your village," it said. "They failed to aid me in time of trouble. Some of your villagers, in fact, refused to believe in my very existence."

Mei-lan looked up at the dragon. "I know they did wrong," she said, "but they are not wicked people. Most of them knew nothing about this. There are babies and little children in our village who never hurt anybody. Oh, please, Great One, do not let the barbarians kill us all."

The dragon was silent, its eyes half closed as though it were listening to some hidden inner voice. "It is always important to help those in need," it said. It reached out a polished golden claw and gently touched Mei-lan's cheek. "Go help your family, Little One," it said softly. "I will see what can be done."

The road leading out of the village was crowded with people, their faces pale with fear. Babies, too frightened to cry, were carried on their mothers' backs. Old men pushed two-wheeled carts piled high with kettles, pots, and pillows. One woman carried the family's prize pig; another carried a round straw basket containing a fat hen and her six yellow chicks. Mei-lan saw the doctor go by, carried in a lacquered chair on poles by four terrified servants, and the mayor, riding a fine white horse with silk ribbons in its tail and a jade-studded leather bridle.

Suddenly a great cry rose from the back of the crowd. "Faster!" someone shouted. "Faster! Run faster! The Mongols are upon us!"

The mayor set his spurs in the sides of his whinnying white horse. "Save yourselves!" he bellowed, as he galloped frenziedly forward. "Run for the hills!"

Mei-lan looked behind her. There in the distance a great black cloud rolled threateningly along the ground, advancing swiftly toward the helpless villagers. It was a cloud of dust, thrown up by the pounding hooves of horses, the steeds of the fierce Northern invaders. As they thundered closer, the sun glinted off the spikes of their steel helmets and the murderous points of their spears. The villagers could hear the clank and rattle of swords and the gleeful shouts of approaching victory.

It was hopeless, Mei-lan realized. The villagers could not possibly outrun their deadly mounted pursuers. She looked at her mother, clutching Little Peach in her arms, and at her father, who, thrusting Plum Boy behind him, was pulling an ax out of his bundle. All around her, people were shrieking and wailing in terror. The noise of hooves and the wild cries of the riders grew louder and louder. "They'll slaughter us all!" someone screamed. "We're all going to die!"

Mei-lan closed her eyes. "Oh, please, Honorable Dragon," she whispered, "oh, please, come now."

And as she stood there, her eyes squeezed tightly shut, the sounds changed.

The shouts of the invaders stopped, replaced by gasps and cries of surprise and shock. The drumming rhythm of the charging hooves faltered, slowed, and came to a halt. All around her, one by one, the villagers fell silent, except for one long indrawn breath of wonder.

Slowly Mei-lan opened her eyes. Then she, too, gasped in awe. There in the sky above their heads loomed the great dragon, its vast wings outspread, its scales a blinding dazzle of pure sun gold. It threw back its magnificent head and its voice roared and echoed off the hills and mountains: "GO BACK WHERE YOU CAME FROM, ACCURSED, AND TROUBLE US NO MORE!" Then it opened its great jaws and loosed a thunderous sheet of red flame. "BEGONE!" it bellowed, "OR BE DESTROYED!"

The invaders, so brave and bloodthirsty only moments before, gave a great moan of horror and fear. Frantically they wheeled their horses around and, hardly daring to look behind them, fled back the way that they had come. The dust stirred up by their headlong retreat hung in the air. The dragon roared once more, a deep, rolling wave of ground-shaking laughter. Then, golden wings glittering, it descended to the earth and faced the astounded villagers. The dragon studied each one in turn–the mayor and the doctor, the farmers and their children, the woman with her squealing pig, the old men and the babies, Mei-lan and her mother and father, Plum Boy and Little Peach–and the villagers, speechless, stared back. Then, like a field of grain bending before the wind, they all bowed low to the dragon.

Now that the barbarians were gone, the mayor had recovered his dignity. He dismounted from his white horse, adjusted his pale green coat embroidered with swallows and chrysanthemums, brushed people aside, and advanced importantly toward the dragon. "O Great One," the mayor began, but the dragon, with an expression of scorn, waved him aside. Its jade green eyes swept the crowd and rested on Mei-lan.

"Come here, Small Daughter," the dragon said.

Mei-lan set down her bundle and walked forward until she stood at the dragon's feet. The dragon reached out a golden claw and very tenderly smoothed Mei-lan's hair. "This child," the dragon said, "fed me when I was hungry and healed me when I was hurt. She comforted me when I was lonely; she cheered me when I was sad. She saved my life when her elders"–the jade green eyes rested briefly on the mayor, who turned red, and on the doctor, who looked at his feet–"would have left me to die. For her sake, I saved the village." The dragon rose to its full height and flexed its glorious golden wings. Very solemnly, it bowed low to Mei-lan. "Thank you, Small Daughter," the dragon said.

There was a murmur of awe from the villagers. Then the dragon bent its long neck until its head was level with Mei-lan's. Quietly, in a voice that only Mei-lan could hear, it said, "Hold out your hand."

Shyly Mei-lan held out her right hand, palm upward.

The dragon delicately stretched out a golden claw and pricked her hand, precisely in the center. Mei-lan gasped. There was a sharp, stinging pain, then a lovely feeling of spreading warmth. When she looked down at her palm, there was no wound. Instead, shining in the cup of her hand was a tiny indelible pinprick of glowing gold.

"We are bonded," the dragon said softly. "You are a true sister, a Dragon Friend. You will be honored in our memories as long as there are dragons here on earth."

For one last time, the golden claw stroked her hair.

"A long and happy life, Small Daughter," the dragon said. "Remember me."

Then, in a rush of incense-scented wind, the dragon, shining even brighter, rose into the air. For a moment it hovered over the village. Mei-lan, craning her neck upward, saw it nod majestically to the villagers. Then the golden head turned toward her. The dragon smiled and one jade green eye–the right eye, which only she could see–winked. And then, between one breath and another, the dragon was gone."

The children stirred. The dragon stared sadly into the darkness over their heads, as though seeing through the gray stone walls into another place and another time. Suddenly it shook its head, as though waking from a deep dream.

"Did Mei-lan get her cricket back?" Sarah Emily asked.

"Indeed she did," said the dragon. "Indeed she did. That very night Plum Boy brought Moon Singer to her bedside. He put the cricket in its tiny cage into Mei-lan's hands and said, 'I am sorry, Honorable Sister.' And then he burst into tears. So Mei-lan hugged him and told him that if he would like, he could put his sleeping quilt right next to hers so that they could both have Moon Singer chirp them to sleep. . . ."

"She was nicer than I would have been," said Zachary.

"Ah," said the dragon softly. And then, almost as if it were talking to itself, it said, "And from that day on, in that part of China, people continued to value their sons, but their daughters–oh, their daughters–they were treasured."

"What happened to Mei-lan?" asked Hannah. "When she grew up?"

"She became a master weaver," the dragon said. "She was the first woman ever to do so. It was a job traditionally held only by men. But she was very talented. She was particularly known for her silk-screens, which had a pattern of bamboo and golden dragons. One of her screens was even sent to the palace of the emperor, as a wedding gift for his eldest daughter. Some of the older people in the village never approved of Mei-lan, of course. Being the first is always difficult."

The dragon reached out a golden claw and gently touched Hannah's hair.

"It's never easy to lead the way, my dear," the dragon said.

The golden lids began to droop over the jade green eyes and the dragon's head began to sag. The children rose quietly to their feet.

"Dragon," said Hannah softly, "may we see you again?"

The dragon roused itself. "I do need my rest," it said. It yawned sleepily. Its eyes closed, then opened again, glowing green slits in the darkness. "But the others will be eager to meet you," it murmured. The green eyes opened a fraction wider.

"If you could just manage to keep our little meetings private?" it asked, in a slightly stronger voice. "There have been some unpleasant experiences. . . . The unpredictability of the adult world . . ."

"Do you mean hunters?" asked Sarah Emily.

"Hunters," the dragon repeated reflectively. "Hunters. In a way, my dear. Hunters, et cetera."

"That means 'and so on,'" Hannah whispered hastily, before Sarah Emily could ask.

"We won't tell anybody," said Zachary. "We promise."

"Thank you, my dear boy," the dragon said.

The golden head dropped, as the dragon settled

itself more comfortably on the cave floor.

"Do come again soon," the dragon murmured. "It was nice to have visitors. To tell the truth, I have been lonely."

There was a smell of smoke and a dragonish snore. The children began to tiptoe softly backward, toward the cave door.

Hannah, for a moment, lingered behind. "Good night, Honorable Dragon," Hannah whispered.

The dragon stirred in its sleep.

"Good night, Small Daughter," said the dragon.

The children emerged from the cave entrance, blinking their eyes in the sudden dazzle of sunshine. Zachary sat down abruptly on the rock ledge.

"Incredible," he said. "Fantastic. Amazing."

He turned to his sisters. "Did it really happen?"

"It really happened," said Hannah. "To us." Her face was glowing.

Only Sarah Emily was subdued.

"I guess it was stupid of me," she said. "To be so scared, I mean."

Hannah shook her head. "It wasn't stupid at all," she said. "We were all scared at first." And she reached over and gave Sarah Emily a little hug.

Zachary said, "Let's come back tomorrow."

Chapter 6

The Puzzle Box

But the next day it rained. And the next day. And the day after that. The sky was heavy and gray, the color of charcoal or pencil lead. Water thundered on the roof and poured through the gutters. Mother, who was happily involved in *The Secret of Silver House*–the governess had just been discovered, strangled, in the conservatory–was oblivious to the weather, but Hannah, Zachary, and Sarah Emily, who had no such homicidal occupations, were beside themselves. Each morning, as they woke to the roar of rain and more rain, their spirits fell lower and lower.

"We'll *never* get back to Drake's Hill," Hannah moaned in despair.

"I wish we could just sleep through this weather, like Fafnyr," fumed Zachary.

They quickly exhausted all their usual rainy-day activities. They played checkers, Parcheesi, and Monopoly, but they couldn't quite keep their attention on the games; and they read—or tried to read—all their favorite books. They spent one afternoon in the kitchen, helping Mrs. Jones make apple pie. But they spent most of their time in the strange little Tower Room.

"Just wait until you see it, Hannah," Sarah Emily said excitedly as the three children, Zachary clutching the iron key, climbed the dusty back stairs. "It's the most wonderful room. Zachary thinks it was Aunt Mehitabel's when she was a little girl."

"She must have had some reason for sending us the key," Hannah said. "Something she wanted us to find. Something special."

"I think we've already found something special," said Zachary. "A box. A treasure box."

"But we can't open it," said Sarah Emily.

"What does it look like?" asked Hannah eagerly. "Do you think it has something to do with Fafnyr?"

"Come on," said Zachary. "We'll show you."

Carefully he unlocked the door to the Tower Room. He climbed the iron ladder, with the two girls close on his heels, and thrust open the trap door. The children scrambled out onto the wooden floor.

"What a marvelous room," said Hannah, getting to

her feet. "If this were my house, I'd live up here."

She stood at one of the little round windows for a moment, gazing longingly out at Drake's Hill, now rain drenched and wreathed in clouds. Then she rapidly circled the little room, running a finger over the head of the painted wooden doll, tapping the brass gong, lifting one of the pink conch shells and holding it curiously to her ear. "You can hear the ocean," she said.

Sarah Emily picked up a shell, held it to her ear, and listened. Her eyes grew round. "Is it really the ocean?" she asked.

Zachary snickered and Sarah Emily's face fell.

"I guess it was a stupid question, wasn't it?" she said.

"No," said Hannah. "It wasn't. Here, try two shells." She held the second conch shell to Sarah Emily's other ear.

"Now it sounds like *two* oceans," Sarah Emily said.

"It's not really," said Hannah. "I learned in school that all you hear when you listen to a shell is the sound of the blood rushing through the blood vessels in your ear. But it's nicer to pretend that it's the sound of the real ocean. As though the shells were remembering where they came from."

"I'll bet that's why Aunt Mehitabel liked them," said Sarah Emily.

She smiled at Hannah and Hannah smiled back.

Hannah turned back to the bookshelf.

"Look at these old storybooks," she said. "I've read some of these. Here's *The Jungle Book* and *Rebecca of Sunnybrook Farm* and *Pollyanna.* And *The Five Little Peppers and How They Grew.*"

"*Peppers?*" said Sarah Emily. She giggled.

"They were kids," said Hannah. "Their last name was Pepper." She took out the book and opened it. "Look at this," she said, and held the book out to Sarah Emily. There was writing on the first page.

"I can't read that," said Sarah Emily. "It's too squiggly."

Hannah took the book back. "'To my dear niece, Mehitabel,'" she read. "'All best wishes for a happy eleventh birthday. Love from Aunt Elvira.'"

Sarah Emily pulled out *Pollyanna.* She opened it to the first page. "This one has a little sticker in it," she said. "It says, 'This book belongs to Mehitabel Davis.'"

"It's called a bookplate," Hannah said.

She replaced the books on the shelf.

"I thought there would be something about Fafnyr here," she said disappointedly. "A message or a clue. Something to tell us more about him."

Across the room Zachary was pulling open the bottom drawer of the desk. He produced the wooden box.

"This is the box we were telling you about," he said to Hannah. "We can't open it. There's no latch."

Hannah picked up the box and turned it around in her hands, examining it. She stroked the polished top, with its inlaid squares and rectangles of colored woods.

"It's the only thing up here that's really strange," Zachary said. "Everything else is interesting, but sort of ordinary, if you see what I mean. But this box is different."

Hannah set the box on the floor and sat down next to it.

"Maybe this is what Aunt Mehitabel wanted us to find," said Hannah. "Maybe this is why she sent us the key to the Tower Room."

They sat in a circle around the box, turning and tapping it, studying it from every possible angle.

"We could just bash it open with a crowbar," Zachary suggested, "or an ax. I know where Mr. Jones has an ax–out next to the woodpile."

"I'm sure Aunt Mehitabel didn't let us find the box so that we could hack it to pieces," said Hannah.

Zachary ran a hand searchingly over the top of the box.

"There *must* be something here somewhere," he said. "A little knob or a handle . . ."

"Do you know what the box top looks like?" Sarah Emily said suddenly. "It looks like one of those number puzzles–you know, the ones with all the numbered squares in a little frame? You have to slide the squares around until you get the numbers in the right order."

"She's right," said Zachary. "That's just what it looks like."

"Maybe one of the top pieces slides," said Hannah.

Zachary's fingers flashed from square to square, pushing and pulling. "And if one does . . ." He stopped. His fingers had found what they were looking for. A single ebony rectangle in the very center of the box slid forward and locked into place with a sharp click.

"Maybe it's like a combination lock," Zachary said.

"Try opening it now," said Hannah.

The children held their breath. Zachary held the box with both hands and tugged upward on the lid. Nothing happened. The box remained tightly shut.

"There must be more to the puzzle," he said.

"Maybe it takes more than just one piece," said Hannah. She touched the pale yellow square just above the ebony rectangle and moved it downward. It clicked into place.

"Now the next piece," said Zachary excitedly. He moved a cocoa brown square. "And the next. I think we've got it."

Slowly, piece by piece, they rearranged the inlaid

pattern of the box top, clicking each wood block into its new position.

"I'm sure this is right," said Hannah. "See how they're beginning to line up? All the dark ones are forming a sort of zigzag."

"So it really *was* a puzzle," said Sarah Emily. "A puzzle box."

"We'll know in a minute," said Zachary. "This is the last block, the one in the corner. You move it, S. E. This was your idea."

Sarah Emily clicked the last block into position. Zachary reached again for the lid. And this time the box opened.

There were two objects inside. The first was a scroll of paper, tied with a faded blue ribbon. The second was carefully wrapped in an old white silk scarf.

"What *is* this?" said Hannah, fumbling with the silk. Beneath the cloth lay something smooth and slippery and cool, like metal, and sharply curved. As Hannah finally pulled it free of its wrappings, it flashed and glimmered, almost with an inner light of its own, brilliantly gold.

Sarah Emily gasped.

The children stared at each other in astonishment.

Then Zachary said, *"It's a dragon's scale."*

"Fafnyr's," said Sarah Emily, in a startled whisper.

"So Aunt Mehitabel *does* know Fafnyr," Hannah

said. "But when did she meet him? And why is he here?" She reached for the paper scroll and pulled off the blue ribbon. "Let's see what this is."

The children carefully unrolled the scroll, weighting the corners with Aunt Mehitabel's books to keep it from snapping shut again. It was a map. There was a title printed at the top. "'Lonely Island,'" Hannah read, "'by Mehitabel Davis.'"

"Wow," said Zachary.

And Sarah Emily said, "Aunt Mehitabel drew *this?*"

The map was beautiful. It was exquisitely drawn in colored inks. It showed an ocean filled with blue wavy lines. Traveling across it was a three-masted ship with billowing sails and flapping flags. Behind the ship swam a pod of pale blue whales, each spouting a frothy plume of water and air. A compass shaped like a rose was drawn in one corner, and each petal of the rose showed the direction of one of the sixteen winds.

"Sixteen winds," breathed Zachary in awe, leaning over until his nose nearly touched the paper.

Right in the center of the map, drawn large, was a crescent-shaped island, the upper and lower arms of which enclosed a cove. At the mouth of the cove stood–"Our house," said Zachary, staring. "I mean, *this* house." A perfect little Victorian house was drawn there, in such detail that the children could hardly make out the finest lines. The tower was there, in miniature, with an infinitesimal weathervane at its peak, and the garden was surrounded by a tiny inked fence.

At the upper end of the island, in the middle of the top arm of the crescent, was the picture of a rocky hill. In the center of the hill was drawn a tiny golden dragon, perfect, from the individual scales of its back to the webbed wings and the arrow-pointed tail. It had three heads. Two of the heads appeared to be asleep–the eyes were closed–but the third showed bright narrow slits of–"What color is that?" asked Sarah Emily. "Gray?"

"Not green?" asked Hannah.

The mouth was spouting minuscule red flames.

Next to the hill was a printed legend. "'Drake's Hill,'" read Zachary. "And underneath it, in smaller letters, it says, 'Fafnyr's Resting Place.'"

Hannah said, "I think we should write a letter to Aunt Mehitabel."

Hannah sat at the desk. They had found paper, envelopes, and to write with, an old-fashioned pen with a metal nib, the kind you dip in an inkwell. Hannah had been elected to write the letter because she had the neatest handwriting. Now she surveyed the row of ink bottles, reading the labels one by one, and finally selected Emerald Green. She uncapped the bottle, dipped the pen, and carefully wrote:

Dear Aunt Mehitabel,

"Now what?" she asked.

"Ask how she met Fafnyr," suggested Sarah Emily.

"Why didn't she just tell us about him?" asked Zachary. "Why does he live on this island?"

"Does she visit him? Are they friends?"

"Did she mean for us to find the puzzle box?"

"When did she draw the map?"

"Why does she have one of Fafnyr's scales?"

"Wait a minute," said Hannah. "I can't write this fast."

Dear Aunt Mehitabel, the letter finally read,

We are having a wonderful time on the island. We did what your note said and went to Drake's Hill. We met Fafnyr. He asked us to come visit him again. When did you meet Fafnyr? Have you known him a long time? Why is he living on the island?

We also found the puzzle box in the Tower Room, with the dragon's scale and the map.

Please write soon.

Love,

Hannah

Zachary

Sarah Emily

"Let's send it right away," said Zachary impatiently.

Hannah folded the letter, tucked it into the envelope, licked the flap, and smoothed the envelope closed.

"We'll get a stamp from Mother," she said.

"Aunt Mehitabel's sealing wax," said Sarah Emily suddenly. "The seal on the envelope she sent to us back home–I just realized what it was. It was a dragon."

On the fourth day, the rain began to taper off. The downpour became a shower, then a patter, and finally a thin drizzle.

"It's almost over," said Hannah with relief. "I can't stand it if we have to wait much longer."

"We could go out in this," said Zachary. "It's not raining very hard anymore. Let's see if there are any old raincoats around or something. Maybe an umbrella."

"Why, of course there are," said Mr. Jones, when the children asked. "We islanders are always prepared for a little rain. Go check those hooks on the back of the kitchen door. Looked to me like there was some rain gear there just about your size."

The rain gear wasn't quite their size. Sarah Emily's poncho trailed on the ground behind her; Hannah's boots were two sizes too big; and the sleeves of Zachary's mackintosh dangled down past his hands, and its stiff shiny collar rode up uncomfortably over his ears. Nobody cared. It was so glorious, at last, to be out-of-doors and on the way back to Drake's Hill. The children splashed along the little path. Clouds rolled away to the east, and the rain, softer now, made a cheerful plunking sound on their rain hoods and hats. Sarah Emily tilted her head back and caught raindrops on her tongue.

When they reached the vast pile of rocks that crowned the peak of the hill, Hannah kicked off the flopping boots that she wore over her sneakers and tucked them under a low-lying outcrop of rock. "I can't climb in these things," she said.

The children, panting, scrambled upward, rocky step by rocky step, until they reached the topmost stone shelf. Single file, they cautiously circled the shelf, its surface slick and shiny with rainwater, and stepped out onto the wide ledge stretching out over the rain-swept ocean. Before them, dark and dripping, was the entrance to the dragon's cave. They paused before it, suddenly nervous, reluctant to go inside.

"I wish it weren't so dark in there," Sarah Emily said, hanging back. "I'm afraid of the dark."

"Why don't you let her hold your flashlight, Zachary?" Hannah suggested. "That might make her feel better."

Zachary, reaching into his raincoat pocket for the flashlight, firmly shook his head.

"No. It's mine," he said. "She might drop it or break it or something."

"No, she won't," said Hannah. "Come on, Zachary. Don't be so selfish. It won't hurt you to share every once and a while."

But Zachary stubbornly shook his head again.

"I just don't like people fooling with my things," he said. "It'll be all right, S. E. Look, I'll go first. Just follow me."

He switched on the flashlight and the children stepped through the door of the cave. The wavering yellow light threw ghostly shadows on the glistening walls and illuminated the strange shapes of stalactites, gleaming and silvered with water. Bunched closely together, the children moved onward, farther in and farther down. The distinctive scent that they now knew was dragon wafted past their noses: incense, cinnamon, and a crisp smoky smell of burning leaves.

"Fafnyr?" said Hannah tentatively, peering into the dark.

The wandering flashlight beam picked up a sudden flash of gold. There was the sound of a great body shifting on the stone floor, and then, far above them, appeared two glowing slits of bright electric blue. The blue widened into a pair of eyes, the pupils straight black lines like a cat's. Then there was a low hissing sound–a furnace noise–as the dragon softly flamed, and the cave blossomed into light. The second head was awake.

This head's voice was deeper, huskier, than the first.

There was a rumble as the dragon harrumphed, coughed, and cleared its throat. "The friends of my brother, I presume?" the dragon said. It lowered its golden head and peered into each of their faces, the blue eyes glowing even more brightly. "Hannah? Zachary? Sarah Emily?"

The children suddenly found themselves at a loss. Addressing a tridrake was confusing.

"Is *your* name Fafnyr, too?" asked Sarah Emily. "I mean, you're the same but you're different, too. Do you–"

But the dragon interrupted with a majestic nod. "*We* are Fafnyr Goldenwings," it said. "It is *our* name."

Hannah began to apologize. "We don't mean to drip all over your floor," she said, "but it's raining outside. We've been stuck in the house for ages."

The dragon's nostrils flared as it sniffed the air. "Rain from the northwest," it murmured. "Sky water." It coiled and uncoiled its golden tail. "This is my kind of weather."

"I didn't know dragons liked water," said Zachary.

"Ah, yes," the dragon said, almost dreamily. "Ah, yes. Some of us are seafarers."

"Mr. Jones–he lives on the other end of the island," said Zachary. "He's going to teach us how to use a boat."

The dragon nodded approvingly.

"A useful skill," it said. "A fine life. Salt air. Exercise. Good companions. Strange ports and foreign harbors."

"It's just a little boat," said Zachary.

The dragon waved a golden claw. "No matter, lad," it said. "We all begin at the beginning." It blinked and stretched its golden wings. Behind it on the cave wall its shadow suddenly stretched and swelled, looming blackly toward the invisibly distant stone ceiling.

Sarah Emily gave a little gasp.

Hastily the dragon folded its wings again, flattening them neatly along its back.

"I beg your pardon," it said apologetically. "Did I startle you? There is no need to be nervous, I assure you. None at all. None whatsoever."

It squirmed slightly and wiggled its shoulder. "My wing tickled," it said.

"It wasn't you," said Sarah Emily miserably. "It

was your shadow. It looked so huge and black. And it's dark in here, back in the corners. I'm scared of the dark."

"She'd be all right," said Hannah, frowning at Zachary, "if she could hold Zachary's flashlight. Then she could shine the light into the corners when she got nervous and she'd see that there's nothing to be frightened of."

Zachary looked embarrassed.

"I'll shine the light anywhere she wants it," he said crossly. "But I don't like handing out my stuff. I take good care of this flashlight. It's special. It has three colored filters on it and two beams. I got it for Christmas."

The dragon made a soft hissing sound deep inside its chest and its flame flared brighter. The light grew stronger and spread to the farthest edges of the cave.

"Nothing," said the dragon, "is easier for a dragon than dark corners. Is this better?"

Sarah Emily nodded shyly.

The dragon turned its golden head toward Zachary and studied him for a long moment.

Then it finally said, "Perhaps you would like to hear a story?"

"Yes," said Zachary. "Please. I'd love to."

"So would I," said Sarah Emily.

"Please tell it," said Hannah.

The children seated themselves on the cave floor, leaning warmly against the dragon's curled golden tail. As Fafnyr began to speak, they felt again as though the walls of the cave faded away before them, revealing another place and time. First there was a cold touch of salt air and a sound of calling sea gulls, then a sudden chatter of voices, the crackling sound of a wood fire, a homey smell of fresh bread baking. They were seeing the world through someone else's eyes.

CHAPTER 7

Jamie

"Jamie Pritchett," the dragon began, "was an orphan. He would have liked, of course, to have had a mother and father, and perhaps some brothers and sisters, too, and a home of his own, like ordinary boys, but he didn't find being an orphan all that bad. He had been one as long as he could remember. . . .

Ever since Jamie was a baby–found wrapped in a scrap of blue blanket in a laundry basket, Mrs. Bingle said–he had lived in an orphanage in an old house (painted a brave shade of sunshine yellow) on the outskirts of London.

The orphanage was run by Mr. and Mrs. Bingle, who, since they had no children of their own, took in the homeless and unwanted and loved them all dearly. But sometimes it was hard. The house was big and drafty and bits of it were falling down. Mr. Bingle had holes in his boots and patches on his winter coat, and sometimes–no matter how hard Mrs. Bingle tried and how clever she was with the household money–there simply wasn't quite enough porridge to go around. Then Mr. Bingle would make a joke about it and everybody would tighten his or her belt a notch and they would all huddle around the fire in the big front room and pretend to be survivors of a shipwreck on the shores of darkest Africa or valiant explorers heading for the North Pole.

Mr. Bingle told stories, which always began, "This is a tale my granddad told me once, so you can be sure that it is true . . ." (but you never could be sure, what with all the dragons and wizards and unlucky princes turned into salamanders and hedgehogs). And Mrs. Bingle would sing songs, and everybody, from the oldest orphan down to the very youngest baby left just last week on the kitchen doorstep, got a hug and a kiss good night. No matter how many children the old house held, there always seemed to be room for one more. But no two ways about it, sometimes it was hard.

That was why when the sailor stopped by the door one fine spring morning looking for a likely boy for a job, Jamie was allowed to go. The sailor was a big strapping fellow with a red bandanna around his head and a gold ring in his ear. He had a friendly way about him, a warm rich laugh that made you think of brown molasses, and a pair of bright little black eyes. "My captain needs a cabin boy for a run to the Indies," the sailor said, offering Mr. Bingle one of his big bronzed hands to shake and giving Mrs. Bingle a polite nod and a bow. "It's a fine ship, a healthy life, good pay, and he'll be treated as well as if he were the captain's own son. And *he'll have a chance for promotion. Why, I started out as a cabin boy myself, and look at me now–second mate of the* Albatross *and hoping someday to have a ship all me own."*

The Bingles, over Jamie's head, exchanged worried glances. "Why, I don't know," Mrs. Bingle said. "It seems so dangerous and so far from home. . . ."

"None of our lads has ever gone to sea," said Mr. Bingle, shaking his head, "and I hear it's a hard life. . . ."

But Jamie had overheard the Bingles in the kitchen that morning deciding that the time had come to sell the last of Mrs. Bingle's great-grandmother's silver spoons, which they had been saving for a rainy day. So he spoke up for himself, looking the laughing sailor straight in the eye. "I'd like to go, sir," he said.

It was no sooner said than done. The sailor, it seemed, was in a hurry, too rushed even to stay long enough to share the Bingles' dinner. "We sail tomorrow on the morning tide," he said. "Fetch your things, lad."

There wasn't much to fetch. Mrs. Bingle packed Jamie's bundle, putting in his spare shirt, three pairs of red-striped stockings that she had knit herself, and a set of scratchy woolly underwear for cold weather. She gave Jamie a hug, told him always to carry a clean handkerchief, and slipped a twopenny piece, which Jamie knew she really couldn't spare, into his pocket for emergencies. Mr. Bingle shook his hand solemnly and wished him luck.

"Keep all your promises, don't take what doesn't belong to you, and always look after those less fortunate than yourself, and you'll

do well in the world," said Mr. Bingle. "And come home as soon as you can, Jamie. We'll miss you."

Then Mrs. Bingle hugged him again, her eyes filling with tears, and Jamie's last sight of them, as he set off down the road with the sailor to make his fortune, was of Mr. Bingle looking sad, with one hand upraised, Mrs. Bingle mopping her eyes with her calico apron, and all the other children crowding around them, calling "Good-bye, Jamie!" "Good luck!" "Come home soon, Jamie!" "Good-bye!"

Jamie and the sailor, whose name, he said, was Black Ben, tramped briskly down the dusty road. "It's ten miles to the harbor, lad; shake a leg," the sailor said, setting a rapid pace on long strong legs. Jamie had to trot to keep up with him, his bundle bouncing up and down against his back. The farther they got from the little yellow house, the less friendly the sailor became. He snapped at Jamie to hurry along when he paused to take a pebble out of his shoe, and called him a foolish brat when he slowed for a moment to admire a blue butterfly perched on a buttercup at the edge of the road. "You'll do no such lollygagging on shipboard," Black Ben growled, jerking him by the arm, "or it will be the worse for you." Jamie began to wish that he'd stayed at home.

He wished it even more when he got his first look at the Albatross. *The ship was old and dirty. It leaned sideways in the water, it was gray and ugly, and it stank. Jamie saw a flick of tiny yellow eyes as a rat peered out from a coil of rope on deck. Jamie hung back as he and Black Ben approached the creaking gangplank, and the sailor gave him a sharp shove between the shoulder blades. "There's more where that came from," the sailor growled, all traces of the warm voice and friendly laughter gone. "Shake a leg, boy!* Move!*" Jamie staggered up the gangplank and boarded the* Albatross.

On deck, the sailors of the ship's crew peered curiously at the new arrival. Two men in ragged striped shirts glanced up from a game of dice, pointed scornfully at Jamie, and sniggered unkindly. A great red-haired giant of a man, with a tattoo of a snarling leopard on his naked chest, called out, "That the captain's new boy, Ben? Looks like fish bait to me!"

"Ah, you'll like the captain fine, boy!" shouted another. "Don't you worry none; he's got a way with young'uns!"

The red-haired man gave a bark of laughter. "Two guineas says the lad doesn't last two days!"

"Done!" bellowed another voice. "Yer on!"

Black Ben gave Jamie another shove, propelling him toward a battered oak door. "Here's the captain's quarters," he said, "where you'll be serving from now on. Look lively, boy!" He knocked on the broad boards. "I've brought the new lad, sir!" he called out, and swung the door open.

The room was dark and sour smelling. The only light filtered in dimly from a grimy porthole set high in one wall. The captain sat at a small table on which stood a bottle of wine, a half loaf of bread, and a hunk of hard yellow cheese. He was chewing. A great red scar ran down his cheek, vanishing into his scraggly beard. There were bread crumbs in the beard. He wore a dirty blue coat with tarnished brass buttons, grubby black breeches, and a pair of tall black boots. The hilt of a knife protruded from the right-hand boot and another knife, with a wide-curving blade, was thrust through his belt. He grinned evilly at Jamie, displaying broken yellow teeth. "What's 'is name?" he asked.

Black Ben cuffed Jamie on the ear. "The captain's speaking to ye!" he said. "Speak up sharp, now!"

"J-Jamie Pritchett, s-sir," Jamie stammered.

"So you want to go to sea, eh, laddie?" The captain grinned, taking a swig from the wine bottle and wiping his mouth with the back of his hand. "You want to sail on the old Albatross, *eh?"*

Jamie was just building up the courage to say, "No, thank you, sir, I'd much rather go back home," when another voice chimed in from a dark corner of the cabin, behind a tattered velvet curtain hanging at the end of the captain's bunk.

"Run!" *it squawked.* "While you have the chance! Run! While you have the chance! Run!"

It might have been his own thoughts shouting aloud. Jamie jumped in surprise, his heart pounding. The captain cursed, thrust back his chair, reached out a long arm, and snatched aside the curtain. The warning screech was the voice of a bird, a scruffy green-and-red parrot with bright yellow eyes, chained by one leg to a metal perch.

"Shut up, you flea-bitten scum!" the captain roared, and struck the parrot with his fist. Shrieking, it fell backward off its perch in a flurry of feathers. As it fell, Jamie suddenly felt the floor of the cabin shift and bob beneath his feet.

The Albatross *had put to sea. There was no going home now.*

Chapter 8

The Voyage of the Albatross

Jamie was tired. He was always tired these days. There was never any time to sit down. It seemed that he barely climbed into his hammock at night before some booted foot was kicking him awake, shouting at him to move his lazy bottom because there was work to be done. Everyone had chores for him to do. There were floors and pots to scrub, barrels to mend, boxes to haul, buckets to empty, sails to stitch, and endless sacks of potatoes to peel. He had to make the captain's bunk, polish his boots, sharpen his knives, serve his meals, and care for his parrot, whose name was Ernestine. Ernestine was Jamie's only friend on board the Albatross, *except for the ship's cat.*

The ship's cat was thin and black, with one white paw. Jamie called him Beetle because he scuttled about the deck like a bug, hiding behind ropes and barrels, taking care to keep out of the sailors' way. When the sailors spotted him, which was seldom, they threw bottles at him. Sometimes they threw bottles at Jamie too. Jamie liked Beetle. He felt that he and the cat were kindred spirits, companions in adversity–though Beetle, Jamie thought, was certainly less fortunate than he was. Beetle had never had a home at all. Whenever he could, Jamie saved bits of dried beef for Beetle from his meager dinner. Sometimes, late at night, the black cat would leap up into Jamie's hammock and lie next to the boy, purring and kneading him with his paws, keeping him warm.

Without Ernestine and Beetle, Jamie's life at sea would have been pure misery. And the more Jamie learned about the Albatross, *the unhappier he became. As he watched and listened, he became certain that this was no ordinary trading voyage to the islands of the Indies. Each day, morning and afternoon, the captain mounted the poop deck, spyglass in hand, and scanned the horizon, searching, ever searching, while the crew seemed to hold its collective breath, each man straining his eyes in one direction and then another, waiting.* For what? *Jamie wondered, and in spite of himself, he found his eyes straining and searching too.* Sea monsters? Whales?

Finally, one afternoon as he worked at peeling potatoes in the ship's galley, his curiosity became too much for him. The cook, a fat bald sailor in a greasy red shirt, sometimes liked to talk. Jamie risked a question.

"Please, sir," he asked, "what is everybody keeping a lookout for?"

The cook growled. "None o' yer business, boy," he rasped. "The captain has his reasons."

Disappointed, Jamie bent his head over the bucket of potatoes.

Then the cook relented. "There's a ship out after our captain," he confided, "an old mate it is, who thinks our captain did him wrong. They fought in the old days, the story goes, and our captain left him for dead and made off with his gold. But he wasn't dead, not by half, and he's been after the captain's blood ever since. Red Jack, his name is. A ship with red sails, he's got, red as blood, and we hear tell that he's threatened to burn the Albatross *to the water line if ever he crosses her path. It's Red Jack the captain's looking for."*

The cook gave a sudden evil-sounding laugh. "At least part o' the time."

"What about the rest of the time?" Jamie asked.

But the cook refused to say more.

The answer soon became clear. One day–a bright clear day, with the sky and the sea the same deep shade of blue–the lookout in the crow's-nest screamed out in excitement, "There she is! Captain! There she is! A sail! A sail! To the northwest! A sail!"

The ship erupted into wild activity. The captain burst from his cabin and flung himself against the rail, training his spyglass on a distant glimmer of white. He squinted for a moment, craning his neck forward, and then turned to the crew and grinned. "It's her all right," he said. "His Majesty's payroll ship, loaded with gold, bound for the colonies." He put the spyglass to his eye again. "She's armed," he said, "but unsuspecting. Raise a signal flag, men–signal that we need help. Let's lure her in."

Jamie's jaw dropped. "But that's not an enemy ship!" he gasped, afraid to believe his ears. "That's one of ours!"

"Not one of ours,*" a burly deck hand said, testing the blade of a cutlass on his thumb. "That's floating plunder, boy. That's the ship will make us all rich, lords in London every one of us, and me with a gold watch and chain, a carriage all trimmed in red leather, and a team of fine black horses."*

"Here she comes," a one-eyed sailor spoke up, grinning. "Floating along innocent as a rose, thinking we're here all hurt and helpless, and when she gets within range . . . ," he paused, made a deathly gargling noise and a gesture of slitting his throat.

"And no one left to tell tales."

"Down to Davy Jones's locker, every last one of them."

Jamie's voice trembled. "You can't!" he cried. "That's murder!"

A hand gripped his shoulder roughly as Black Ben strode by. Jamie winced in pain. "Shut up, boy, and mind your business!" snapped Ben. "All quiet! Ready your weapons!

Let her move in!”

The doomed ship drew nearer and nearer. Its sails gleamed in the sunlight. Jamie could see the men bustling about on her deck, the red-and-blue flag snapping in the wind, the carved figurehead–a green-tailed mermaid with flowing golden curls–and the name painted on the side: The Sea Lady. *The captain –Jamie thought it must be the captain in a blue hat with a gleaming gold cockade–raised a spyglass to his eye and aimed it toward the* Albatross. *Jamie felt as though it rested directly on him. Closer and closer the ship came. The men of the* Albatross *tensed, cannon loaded, swords and pistols in their hands, awaiting their captain's order.*

Jamie could stand it no longer. He sprang to the rail and hauled himself up, waving an arm in the air, and shouted at the top of his voice, “Turn back! Turn back! *There are pirates here!* Pirates! *Turn back!” At first he thought that his warning had gone unnoticed. Then he saw a change: the captain barking orders, seamen leaping to the rigging, the ship beginning to turn.*

On the Albatross, *the captain bellowed in fury.*

"They may not be out of range!" howled Black Ben. "Fire all cannons! Now! Fire!"

The guns roared and spat red flames. Cannonballs sped across the water, deadly balls of blackened metal, enough to cripple a ship and leave it broken and drifting, sinking in the water. But the cannons roared too late. The cannonballs fell short, plopping harmlessly, like pebbles, into the bright blue waves. The trap had failed. The Sea Lady *had escaped.*

"Where is that blasted brat?" *the captain screamed. His boots thundered on the boards of the deck.* "You misbegotten little rat!" *Purple faced with rage, he snatched Jamie up by his shirt collar and shook him, then hurled him violently against the mast. Jamie's head crashed against unyielding wood. Everything went black.*

CHAPTER 9

The Treasure-Trove

When Jamie awoke, he was lying on sand. At first, he had no idea where he was. "I'm dead," he thought, "or dreaming." His head ached, and when he raised his fingers to his temple, he felt a lump the size of a goose egg, crusted with blood. It hurt to touch. Slowly he opened his eyes and found that it was dark. Stars glittered in the sky above him. A full yellow moon cast a shining yellow path on the water and silhouetted a ship, sails furled, floating silently at anchor. "We've landed somewhere," thought Jamie.

Something stirred at his side and he felt a warm furry presence: Beetle, snuggled up against his hip. He stroked the black cat's ears and Beetle, thankful that Jamie was awake at last, purred. When Jamie lifted his head, he saw that he lay on a stretch of smooth sandy beach bordered by rocky cliffs topped with trees. Two longboats were pulled up on shore, their oars resting in the oarlocks. Thirty yards down the beach he saw the orange glow of a fire, surrounded by moving black figures, and heard the clink of bottles, shouts, and snatches of song. The pirates were consoling themselves for the loss of the Sea Lady.

Slowly Jamie sat up. He was bruised and sore, but–he wiggled his arms and legs–no bones were broken. He scratched Beetle underneath the chin. "I sure am glad you managed to come along, old fellow. What did you do, sneak on board the boat?" Beetle closed his eyes and purred.

Jamie glanced toward the pirates' fire. Someone threw something on it that made the flames blaze up blue, and there was a deep shout of laughter. Jamie stroked the cat again. "Let's get a little closer and see if we can find out what's going on."

Silently, boy and cat crept across the sand and huddled behind a jumbled pile of driftwood. Jamie, peeking cautiously through the twisted branches, found himself staring directly at the back of the captain's head. On the opposite side of the fire, three seamen clanked their mugs together and began a faltering song about life on the ocean waves. One of the singers kept hiccupping and forgetting the words.

From the captain's right came the voice of Black Ben.

"What d'ye plan to do with the brat, Captain?"

The captain drank deeply from a squat brown bottle. "We'll leave the little rat here," he snarled. "He'll not set foot on my ship again."

A hoarse voice from the other side of the fire shouted, "Hang him from the yardarm!"

"Feed him to the sharks!" roared another.

The captain drank again.

"Forget the brat," he bellowed. "We'll leave him here to starve. Sing, lads! Sing!"

Jamie, crouched behind the wall of driftwood, smoothed Beetle's soft ears. "They're planning to abandon me," he whispered softly to the cat. "It's called being marooned. They're angry because I warned away the other ship. Well, that's fine with me. We're going to get out of here, Beetle. We're going to abandon them.*"*
Jamie, unnoticed, got to his feet. Silently he and Beetle slipped away, like shadows in the moonlight, toward the cliffs.

There they found a small sandy path, leading sharply upward. They climbed, Jamie soon panting, Beetle bounding at his heels. At the top, they paused and peered down–far down–over the edge, to the beach. The fire had shrunk to a prickle of red embers; silent lumps around it were the forms of sleeping pirates. A few hardy souls were still awake, singing a song about a dead man's chest and a bottle of rum.

"Good riddance," muttered Jamie to

himself, and Beetle rubbed against his leg in agreement. Together, they turned away from the cliff's edge and followed the path on into the woods. A full moon lit their way, turning the rocks and trees to silver. They walked on and on, glad to be on land again and free.

Once, they saw an owl pass, silent winged above the path, and heard the rustle of a field mouse diving for cover. Once, a pair of rabbits, surprised eyes round as saucers, rose on their hind legs to watch them pass. Finally, as Jamie's eyes began to droop with tiredness, the trees gave way to a wide shelf of rock, still warm from the day's sunshine. Jamie sat down. "Let's just rest for a minute, Beetle," he murmured, and was almost instantly asleep. Beetle settled down in his lap. His eyes closed too.

They were awakened hours later by a shaft of sunlight and the chatter of birds. Jamie lay peacefully, basking in the warmth, stroking Beetle's fur. "First of all, we'll have to find out where we are," he told the cat happily, "and then we'll figure out how to get home. You'll like having a home, living with the Bingles and all the rest of us. Mrs. Bingle loves cats; she says a kitchen without a cat is like stew without salt."

Beetle purred as if he understood.

"And to find out where we are," Jamie continued, "we'll have to find some people. Nice people, who might share their breakfast. I'm hungry, Beetle, aren't you?"

*Beetle gave a meow of agreement, hopped off Jamie's lap, and began to prowl. He jumped to the path and back up to the shelf of rock, leaped to a ledge above Jamie's head and dropped back down, and then sidled around a rocky corner and vanished. When he didn't reappear, Jamie, curious, followed him. Around the corner was a broad opening like an entryway, its edges rubbed shiny as though by some large animal passing in and out–*What could be that big? *Jamie wondered. Beetle had found a cave.*

The minute Jamie stepped through the entrance, he realized that here was no ordinary animal's lair. His first impression was a dazzling explosion of color: ruby red, emerald green, sapphire blue, diamonds shooting rainbow rays, the icy sparkle of silver, and the warm glow of gold. The cave was a treasure-trove. Riches lay as far as the eye could see. Golden goblets studded with gems lay in heaps; jeweled swords were propped against the rocky walls. There were mountains of gold coins, a jumble of gleaming crowns, piles of necklaces, rings, jeweled belts, and bracelets. Jamie picked up a coin and rubbed it between his fingers: It bore the portrait of an ancient queen and a legend in a strange language.

He opened a wooden chest and found it full of cut gems. He let a handful trickle glitteringly through his fingers. Just a pocketful–half a pocketful–would keep Mr. and Mrs. Bingle and their brood safe and comfortable for the rest of their lives. Just half a pocketful. "No one would know," Jamie thought to himself. "Maybe no one lives here anymore. Maybe no one even owns this treasure." He reached out toward the chest, hesitated, and then drew his hand back. Mr. Bingle's kindly face rose up before his eyes and Jamie seemed to hear his voice: Keep all your promises, don't take what doesn't belong to you, and always look after those less fortunate than yourself, and you'll do well in the world–and come home as soon as you can, Jamie. We'll miss you.

Jamie stood frozen for a moment. Don't take what doesn't belong to you *seemed to echo in his head. He sighed regretfully and his hands dropped to his sides. "Come on, Beetle," he said. "This isn't ours and we're trespassing. Let's get on our way."*

As they stepped out of the cave, they heard voices, shouts–"This way, I tell you! See the tracks?"–and the rapid thudding of boot heels on stone.

"Why?" One voice rose above the others.

"Because the captain wants him back, that's why. He doesn't want to leave him behind, after all. He's got other plans for him. Is that reason enough for you?"

Jamie went cold with fear. He crouched, trembling, behind the sheltering rock, but it was too late. A shadow fell across his knees.

"And here's our little runaway!" It was Black Ben's voice. "Ripe for the picking, and . . ." The voice stopped dead in astonishment, then rose in a joyous shout. "Lads! Quick, to me! Gold!*"*

Jamie was forgotten. The pirates crowded past him, fighting and shoving to enter the cave. Their cries of glee echoed off the metal-stacked walls. "What shall we put it in?" someone shouted.

"Sacks!" another voice answered. "I've found some sacks!"

"Pack them full, lads!" It was Black Ben

again. "We'll make a trip to the beach and come back for the rest. Look lively, now!" He emerged from the cave, smirking, a diamond tiara on his head, his pockets sagging with coins. "Maybe you had thoughts of keeping this all to yourself, Jamie, me boy? I don't envy you when the captain finds out; on me soul, I don't. And him in a bad mood already, having lost the Sea Lady.*" He shook his head and chuckled. "A poor day's work for you, I'd say. The captain will feed you to the little fishes when I tell him, mark me words. You'll be walking the plank before sundown!" And he laughed again.*

Then the laughter stopped abruptly as, startled, he looked toward the sky. An immense black shadow had blotted out the sun. There was a rush of wind, a strange sweet smell of incense, wood smoke, and cinnamon, and a vast whump of wings. Black Ben's mouth fell open and his eyes bulged wide with horror. The owner of the cave had come home.

It was a dragon. Its massive body was coin gold; its great webbed wings sparkled brilliantly in the sun. It had three heads, Jamie noticed in astonishment. Two, nestled on its shoulders, appeared to be sound asleep. The third, arched high above them on a soaring golden neck, glared at the intruders with piercing blue eyes. The dragon spat a sheet of flame, blackening the rock above the cave door. The head turned slowly toward Black Ben.

"Empty your pockets," the dragon rasped, in a voice filled with angry menace. "Remove my crown."

Ben, shaking, pulled off the diamond tiara and flung it back into the cave. He pulled his pockets inside out and gold and silver coins cascaded in a pile around his feet. Behind him, from the cave, came a series of crashes and clatters: The pirates inside were rushing to divest themselves of their stolen loot. They stumbled out into the open, their pockets hanging out, their hands empty.

"Leave–my–cave," *the dragon said, in a fiery hiss, "and, if you value your miserable lives, never return again." It tilted back its head and roared.*

Black Ben turned pale with fear, pushed past Jamie, and ran. His men, terrified, followed. Their boots could be heard on the path, picking up speed, receding into the distance. Only Jamie and Beetle were left behind.

The dragon swiveled its golden neck and

turned its sea blue gaze toward Jamie. Jamie's knees grew weak with fear and his heart thundered in his chest. Beetle, cowering against Jamie's ankles, whimpered.

The dragon changed color slightly. It seemed, for a moment, to turn faintly pink. "Please, don't be frightened, young man," it said. It cleared its throat in an embarrassed fashion. Then it said, looking at a point just above Jamie's head, "I fear I lost my temper."

Jamie took a deep breath. He leaned down and gave Beetle a reassuring pat.

"That's all right, sir," he said to the dragon.

The dragon shook its golden head. "A dragon's hoard," it said defensively, "is private. When I saw those . . . disreputable persons . . . meddling with my prized collection, I quite lost my head."

"It's a wonderful collection," Jamie said. "I've never seen such treasure."

The dragon attempted to look modest. It waved one wing in a dismissing gesture.

"Not a bad start," it said consideringly. "But then, I haven't been hoarding as long as some. It takes centuries to accumulate a truly impressive hoard. Why, I've seen some hoards, young man, that make this"–it *nodded toward the cave—"look piddling."*

The dragon snorted, releasing a small cloud of blue smoke.

"Piddling," it repeated.

"It's truly beautiful, sir," Jamie said, "so many jewels and so much gold. But I don't understand what it's all for. What do you do *with all that treasure?"*

"Do?" *the dragon repeated, in shocked tones.* "Do? *One does not* do *things with a hoard, young man. One* has *it. One adds to it. Sometimes one rearranges it. But one does not* do *anything with it. That's not what a hoard is for."*

Jamie bit his lip. "That seems sort of selfish," he said.

The blue eyes narrowed. The dragon was ominously silent.

Jamie stumbled on. "Just one of those jewels would help so many people. Mr. and Mrs. Bingle—they're like a father and mother to me, since I don't have any of my own—they've given away everything they have to take care of children that nobody else wanted. And you're just sitting on this mountain of diamonds. It doesn't seem right."

"A hoard is a private *collection," the dragon*

said. "You don't understand, young man. One does not share *a hoard."*

Jamie said nothing.

"It is the nature *of dragons to hoard," the dragon said uncertainly.*

"Once, at home, at Christmas time," Jamie said, "we had pieces of gingerbread. It was a special treat, but there weren't enough pieces for everyone to have one all his own. We were supposed to share. But I didn't. I took a whole piece for myself and went and hid under the stairs and ate every crumb. Later I felt awful. And Mr. Bingle said . . ."

"That cookies don't count?" the dragon asked hopefully.

"No," Jamie said. "That it was selfish. I knew it was wrong but I did it anyway. Mr. Bingle said that I had succumbed to temptation."

There was a doleful pause. The dragon hung its head.

"You are right," it said, after a moment. "Hoarding is selfish. Unspeakably so." It miserably shuffled its golden claws. "I can't think what came over me," the dragon said. "I, too, have succumbed to temptation. I have been petty and foolish."

Then it said, in a much smaller voice, "I am ashamed."

"So am I, sir," Jamie said. He looked down at his feet. "In your cave . . . it wasn't just the pirates. I meddled with your collection too. I wanted to take some of your treasure. I almost did."

"But you didn't," the dragon said.

Jamie opened his mouth to speak again, but the dragon held up a silencing claw.

"I, too, was properly brought up," it said. "Father had very strict opinions about hoarding."

For a moment the dragon managed to look small and guilty.

"Very strict," the dragon said. It gulped nervously.

Jamie gave a sympathetic nod.

Suddenly the dragon leaned forward and gazed deeply into Jamie's eyes. It studied him for a long moment. Jamie felt as though the dragon were reading his mind, turning over all his thoughts and dreams, one by one.

"Keep all your promises," *it murmured.* "Don't take what doesn't belong to you, and always look after those less fortunate than yourself. *Precisely. Father himself couldn't have said it better."*

The dragon took a deep breath, lifted its chin, and squared its shoulders.

"You have set a good example, young man," the dragon said. It glanced disgustedly toward the entrance to the hoard. "You have brought me to my senses." It made a harrumphing noise deep in its throat. "I am inexpressibly grateful."

Then it said, very solemnly, "Please hold out your hand."

Jamie, bewildered, held out his right hand. The dragon stretched out a curved claw and pricked Jamie's palm, precisely in the center. Jamie felt a sharp sting, like a bee sting, followed by a wonderful feeling of warmth. There, gleaming in the middle of his hand, was a tiny fleck of glowing gold.

"We are bonded," the dragon said. "You are a true Dragon Friend."

"You've been my friend, too," Jamie said. "You saved Beetle and me from the pirates."

Then Jamie reached out and very gently touched the dragon's golden claw. "Please, sir," he said, "could you help me get back home?"

⁂

Sarah Emily stirred and rubbed her foot, which had fallen asleep. "So what happened?" she asked. "Did you take him home?"

"I felt it would have been unwise," the dragon said, "to put in a personal appearance. The populace would have been unduly alarmed."

"So what did you do?" asked Hannah.

"I lit a signal fire," said the dragon, "on the cliffs. It burned for eight days and eight nights, and on the morning of the ninth day, a ship came into view. It was the *Sea Lady,* and the crewmen remembered Jamie. 'The gallant lad from the pirate ship,' they called him. They took Jamie and Beetle away. They never knew I was there."

"What happened to the pirates?" asked Zachary. "Did they just escape?"

The dragon gave a wicked reminiscent smile. "The sailors on the *Sea Lady,"* it said blandly, "had a strange tale to tell. There, in the middle of the ocean, they came upon the smoldering wreckage of a ship. A message was pinned with a dagger to the broken mast: 'So perish the enemies of Red Jack!' Not a soul on board was left alive . . ."

"So their old enemy caught up with them," said Zachary. "Serves them all right!"

"Except a parrot, clinging to a floating spar. They took the parrot with them . . ."

"Ernestine!" cried Sarah Emily.

"And Jamie took her home with him and Beetle. The captain of the *Sea Lady* took quite an interest in Jamie, since Jamie had saved his life and those of all his men. Eventually he recommended Jamie for a commission in the Royal Navy, and Jamie became a sea captain. His ship was called the *Golden Dragon.*"

"But how did the Bingles manage?" asked Zachary. "They must have been happy to have Jamie back safe, but weren't they still poor?"

The dragon looked embarrassed. "Hoarding is a sad fault," it said. "A responsible dragon struggles to overcome it."

"So you gave him some of the treasure?" asked Hannah.

The dragon gave a little cough. "Jamie Pritchett," it said, "went home with a bulging sack of gold and jewels. Mr. and Mrs. Bingle and their adopted family lived happily ever after. There was money to mend the roof and to put pudding and roast beef on the table; at Christmas, there were presents for all; and Mrs. Bingle, who had been thin with worry, even managed to grow a little plump. . . ."

"What happened to the rest of the hoard?" asked Zachary.

"I gave it up," the dragon said. "I gave it away."

"Weren't you sorry," Zachary asked, "to lose your private collection?"

The dragon leaned forward and looked deeply into Zachary's eyes. It studied him, unblinking, for several long moments. Then it nodded briskly, as though it had learned all there was to know about Zachary and had reached some important decision. Finally it answered Zachary's question.

"No," the dragon said. "I wasn't sorry. It felt better. It was the right thing to do."

It extended a gleaming golden claw and tapped Zachary companionably on the shoulder. "You'll see," it said.

Suddenly the dragon gave an enormous yawn. "Well," it said, "this has certainly been delightful." It yawned again. "Do come back when you can for another visit. We look forward to your return." The sea blue eyes drooped sleepily and closed.

Then they flickered back open.

"If you could preserve your admirable reticence?" it murmured. "About our meetings? Things can be so difficult these days. . . ."

"He means don't talk about him to anybody," Hannah whispered to Sarah Emily. "He wants us to keep him a secret."

"Of course we can keep a secret," Sarah Emily said.

"You can count on us, Fafnyr," said Zachary.

The glowing eyes closed again. The light in the cave dimmed.

"Good night, Fafnyr," Hannah whispered. The children turned and quietly tiptoed away through the rapidly darkening cave.

Zachary reached into his raincoat pocket and pulled out his flashlight.

"Here, S. E.," he said. He switched on the light and pressed it into Sarah Emily's hand. "You carry it. It does make you feel better when you're scared of the dark."

It was too dim to see Sarah Emily's face, but he could almost feel her smile.

"Oh, Zachary," Sarah Emily said. "Thank you."

CHAPTER 10

Sister

The summer days slid by. The children chafed to return to Drake's Hill.

"But we shouldn't go too often," Zachary warned. "People might get suspicious."

Sarah Emily nodded. "We promised to keep Fafnyr a secret," she said.

"We'll wait a while," Hannah said. "Until it's absolutely safe."

Mr. Jones brought the mail every day from the mainland: *Astronomy* magazine for Zachary, a letter to Mother from her publisher, a note in a flowered envelope to Hannah from Rosalie. But nothing came from Aunt Mehitabel.

"Why doesn't she write?" Hannah fretted.

"Maybe tomorrow," said Zachary hopefully.

But still no letter came.

As they waited impatiently until they felt it was safe to visit Drake's Hill, they struggled to find ways to pass the time. Nothing worked very well. Hannah spent afternoons in the Tower Room, eating apples and reading Aunt Mehitabel's old storybooks. Zachary went with Mr. Jones to dig clams and dragged out the telescope on clear nights to view the rings of Saturn and the moons of Jupiter. Father came for a visit and took the children on a trip to a marine biology laboratory on the mainland, where Zachary was nipped by a lobster and Sarah Emily petted a horseshoe crab. Mother finished her book. Mrs. Jones taught the children how to make oatmeal cookies, and Mr. Jones taught them how to row the boat. They went swimming in the sunny waters of the little cove below the boathouse.

Finally, a scribbled postcard arrived from Aunt Mehitabel. "Delighted to hear from you," the card read. "Unexpectedly called out of town. Long letter later. Give my regards to F."

"F," Sarah Emily said. "Fafnyr."

Zachary reached out and took the card from Hannah's hand.

"There's a P.S.," he said. "In tiny letters down at the bottom. It says, 'Don't forget to use your heads.'"

"What does *that* mean?" asked Sarah Emily.

"This is awful," said Hannah in dismay, as Zachary

dropped the postcard on the table. "She didn't tell us *anything.*"

"I can't stand this waiting any longer," said Sarah Emily.

"Neither can I," said Zachary. "It's been days and days. Let's go see Fafnyr."

"Let's," said Hannah. "I'm sure it's safe by now."

"And let's take the boat," said Zachary. "We can say we're going to row along the shore toward the north end of the island to picnic on the beach. Then we can walk from there to Drake's Hill."

"Of course you may," said Mother, when asked, "but remember the rules: Stay close to shore, stay together, and wear your life jackets."

Mrs. Jones helped them pack a picnic basket. There was a thermos of lemonade, apples, oatmeal cookies, cucumber pickles, hard-boiled eggs, and packets of peanut-butter-and-banana sandwiches. "Enough food for an army," Sarah Emily said.

Zachary took first turn at the oars. It was a beautiful day and the water was calm and blue. Hannah chanted "Row, Row, Row Your Boat," and then "Anchors Aweigh" and "My Bonnie Lies Over the Ocean." Gulls circled overhead and the wind lifted the children's hair.

"You're awfully quiet, S. E.," Hannah said. "What's the matter?"

Sarah Emily, sitting in the bow of the boat, turned toward her brother and sister.

"Look how deep the water is," she said. "There could be anything down there. Even right under the boat. Sharks or giant octopuses or some huge sea monster. What if we tipped over?"

"Oh, come on," said Zachary. "Stop fussing. Look how close to shore we are. And you can swim. You won that ribbon in the swim race at camp last summer."

"Second place," said Sarah Emily. "I wasn't very good."

"You always say that," Zachary said.

"No sea monster could possibly come in this close to land," said Hannah. "It would scrape its stomach on the bottom."

Sarah Emily still looked worried.

"Anyway, this is as far as we're going," said Zachary. "Look, there's Drake's Hill. Let's land and eat lunch."

He turned the boat toward shore. As they reached the shallows, Hannah jumped out and helped haul the boat up onto the sand. Zachary carefully turned the oars and propped them on the stern seat. Hannah lifted out the picnic basket.

"I'm starving," she said. "Let's eat right now. Mrs. Jones even packed a blanket for us to sit on."

The children spread the blanket on the sand. Zachary began to unpack the food. Hannah poured lemonade into paper cups.

Presently, Zachary, his mouth full of hard-boiled egg, said in a muffled voice, "I can't wait to see Fafnyr."

"Me either," said Hannah, finishing the pickles. "It seems like forever."

"I hope he's awake," said Sarah Emily.

Hannah frowned. "He always woke up before," she said.

Zachary hastily gulped his oatmeal cookie.

"Let's hurry," he said.

The children scrambled the leftovers back into the picnic basket, shook the sand out of the blanket, folded it, and carried the picnic things back to the boat.

"Put your sneakers on," said Hannah. "You can't climb Drake's Hill barefoot."

The children set off across the beach, then up a rocky slope to a wide grassy field dotted with black-eyed Susans and Queen Anne's lace. Across the field, dark against the bright blue sky, rose Drake's Hill. Excitedly, all three started to run.

They reached the hill, climbed up the rocky ledges–easier now that they knew all the handholds and footholds–and edged cautiously around the stone shelf to the entrance to Fafnyr's cave. Again, the ocean spread out before them, blue, green, and glittering. From the sea came the briny scent of salt water, from behind them, the magical scent of cinnamon, incense, and bonfire smoke–the elusive odor that they now knew as "dragon." Silently, one by one, they slipped through the entrance and into the cave.

"It seems rude to barge right in without knocking," whispered Sarah Emily. "What if he's sleeping? Or he just doesn't want to be disturbed?"

A slithering, shifting sound came from the back of the cave, then a soft hiss as a dragon flare blossomed in the darkness. The third dragon head stared at them with cool metallic silver eyes.

"*She,*" the dragon said pointedly, "is awake."

"I'm sorry," Sarah Emily said. "I didn't mean . . ."

"Two brothers and a *sister,*" Hannah whispered. "Fafnyr told us on our first visit, remember?"

"It's just that it's funny to think of a dragon as a girl," said Zachary.

The dragon snorted. "*We* are both male and female," the silver-eyed head said snappishly. "*Female,* young man, not *girl.* And I'll thank you to remember it."

"I will," said Zachary hastily. "Ma'am."

The dragon inclined its head. It managed somehow to look like the portrait of Queen Victoria in

Hannah's world history textbook: regal and unamused.

"Jumping to conclusions," the dragon said, in a schoolroom tone, "is a characteristic human fault. The thoughtless assumptions, the inability to see what's before one's very eyes . . ." Its voice trailed off. It lifted an admonishing golden claw and fixed the children with a sharp silver eye.

"A dragon, on the other hand," the dragon said, "is judicious and observant. Tolerant and generous. Polite. Tidy. Brave. And self-reliant."

Sarah Emily gave a little sigh. The dragon bent its golden head down toward her, gazed at her for a moment, and its eyes softened.

"And you, I understand, are the Last Awake?" it asked gently.

"I'm the youngest," said Sarah Emily. "I'll be nine in November."

The dragon nodded understandingly. Its silver eyes, studying her intently, were kind. "I see," the dragon said. It flexed its golden wings and rearranged itself on the cave floor. "And what do you do best, my dear?" it asked.

Sarah Emily looked flustered. "I'm not really good at much of anything," she said. "I like to read. And I might take piano lessons this fall, but I'm not sure yet. It looks awfully hard."

"A challenging instrument," the dragon said. "But

quite rewarding with practice." It gestured with its claws. "Relaxed wrists," it said.

"S.E. always says she's not good at things," Zachary said, "but it's not really true."

"Mother says it's because of self-esteem," said Hannah. "Sarah Emily doesn't have much, so she's afraid to try new things. Sometimes she won't try to do anything at all."

"It's not that I won't try things," Sarah Emily said defensively. "It's just that everybody else always does things so much better."

"Ah," the dragon said. "I see." For a moment it seemed lost in thought.

Then it turned once more to Sarah Emily, and said, "I once knew a child very much like you, my dear. Very like. Perhaps you would care to hear her story?"

"Please," said Sarah Emily. "Yes, please."

Hannah and Zachary nodded.

"Make yourselves comfortable," said the dragon.

The children curled up at the dragon's feet to listen, and Sarah Emily lay back against the smooth golden tail. Once again, as the dragon spoke, the cave walls seemed to fade and disappear. This time there was a swirl of fluffy clouds, a smell of oil and leather, the rhythmic sound of an engine, a rush of moving wind. They were in another place, living someone else's life, seeing through someone else's eyes.

CHAPTER 11

The Flying Machine

"Hitty and Will," the dragon said, "were on their way around the world. Hitty was ten years old that year, and her brother, Will, was twelve. Will was having a wonderful time, but Hitty worried because they were traveling by airplane–airplanes were still new in those days–and she never really liked to fly. . . .

The little silver plane had been in the air for almost the whole day, ever since taking off in the bright sun of early morning–a lifetime ago, thought Hitty–from a grassy field near San Diego, California. It was the fourth day of their journey. They had flown all the way across America–"From ocean to ocean," said Will proudly–stopping only for food, fuel, and sleep. Now Hitty, Will, and their father were airborne again. Will and Hitty's father was not only a pilot, but a freelance journalist. He wrote magazine and newspaper stories. "This will make a terrific story," Father had said a month ago, when the idea first popped into his mind. "FIRST CHILDREN TO CIRCLE GLOBE BY AIR! I can just see the headlines. You'll both be famous, just like Charles Lindbergh."

"Lindbergh crossed the whole Atlantic with just one ham sandwich to eat," said Will cheerfully. "Let's remember to take more than that. Flying gives me an appetite."

"Now," Hitty thought, looking giddily down at the waves of the blue Pacific far below them, "we're more likely to be famous for something much worse. FIRST CHILDREN TO DISAPPEAR FOREVER, OUT IN THE MIDDLE OF NOWHERE."

The little plane coughed and stuttered, veering uncertainly back and forth across the sky. Father struggled with the controls, his face set in grim, worried lines.

"What's happening?" asked Hitty in a voice that tried to come out brave but, in spite of itself, trembled a little.

"I'm not sure," her father said. "We're losing altitude."

He tried the radio again, which answered with a choking sound and a chatter of static.

The plane continued to drift downward, its engine making a jerky hiccupping noise. Will, sitting next to her, reached over and gripped Hitty's hand. It helped to have Will there. "At least we're all together," thought Hitty miserably, "except for poor Mother, all by herself back home."

Father squared his shoulders and adjusted the goggles that he wore over his leather flying helmet. He's going to tell us that this is it, Hitty thought, her heart beginning to bang painfully against her ribs. It's all over. We're all going to crash into the ocean and die. She squeezed Will's hand harder. But Father said none of those things.

"There's an island down there," Father said. "Just a little scrap of a thing, but I think we can make it. I'll try to set us down on the beach. Then we'll get the radio patched up and somebody will come out to pick us up lickety-split. It'll be all right, you'll see. Hang on, kids. We're going in."

There was a stomach-turning swerve and drop as Father angled the plane over and down, aiming for a miniature green-and-brown speck that Hitty and Will could now see, just bobbing up amid the endless sea of blue. The engine bucked and sputtered. The wings tilted ominously. The whole plane seemed to slide and catch itself, slide and stop, like a sled scraping over rocky ground on its way downhill. "Just hang on," Father kept repeating, as though he were praying. "Just–hang–on–"

Hitty hid her face against Will's shoulder. Then there was one last roller-coaster-like dip and a shuddering thud as the plane hit the sand, followed by a violent jerk and a crash. The plane had swiveled around, skidded, and smashed into a clump of palm trees. Hitty and Will were thrown forward against the pilot's seat. Their father was flung against the windshield. For one endless moment, all three lay perfectly still.

Then Hitty, her head spinning, began to struggle to sit up. Will was on top of her, his elbow in her mouth, his right knee in her stomach. "Will! Are you all right?" she cried.

Will moaned and cautiously rubbed his head. "I think so," he said. "What about you?"

"I don't know," said Hitty, in a shaky voice. "Everything hurts. Where's Father?"

"Can you move your arms and legs?" asked Will. "Come on, Hitty. Try."

Hitty wiggled cautiously, first her arms, then her legs. "I can move everything," she said. "But it still hurts."

"Then there's nothing broken," said Will. "It's just bumps and bruises. Father? Are you all right?"

"Father!" cried Hitty.

There was no answer from the motionless form in the pilot's seat. Will managed to get unsteadily to his feet, leaned forward, and examined their father's still body. "He's breathing," he said, his voice high with relief. "He's breathing, Hitty, he's alive. But his head is bleeding. We'll have to get him out of here and carry him someplace where he can lie down."

Will managed to open the crushed door of the cockpit partway, by beating at it with his foot. It made a metallic screaming sound as it opened, which made Hitty grit her teeth and wince. One after the other, they wriggled through the narrow gap and dropped to the ground.

"Oh, no!" Will gasped in dismay. "We'll never fix that!" The children gazed miserably at the wreckage of the little plane. Great curving marks in the beach sand showed the path *the plane had taken, ending in the trees where it now lay. It was tilted nearly on its side, its wings broken and twisted, its propeller wrenched out of shape, its silver body dented and deformed. Will rubbed his hand across his eyes. "She'll never fly again, Hitty," he said sadly.*

"But how will we get home?" Hitty asked. She sounded frightened and her eyes began to fill with tears.

Will shook his head. "I don't know," he said, "but first we have to get Father out of there. Do you know where there's any rope?"

There was a coil of rope in the little cargo hold in the belly of the plane. "There are all sorts of useful things in here," Will shouted, burrowing headfirst, his legs kicking in the air. "Here, Hitty! Catch! There's a first-aid kit and a couple of blankets." Will emerged, squirming backward, his arms full. He held a tin box of matches, a gallon bottle of fresh water, and a sealed box of soda crackers. "Dinner!" he said, pointing with his chin at the cracker box.

Next, looping the rope over his shoulder, Will climbed back up to the cockpit, followed anxiously by Hitty. Father was still unconscious, his face chalky pale, his eyes closed. The children looped the rope under his arms and knotted it, wrapping the other end firmly around the copilot's seat. "This should hold him steady while we lower him to the ground," Will said. Gasping and straining, they managed to force the crushed cockpit door farther open. As gently as possible, they tugged their father's legs free and swung them around, positioning them so that his feet dangled through the door. Father stirred for a moment and moaned, but his eyes stayed closed. Then, Hitty, steadying from beneath, and Will, manning the rope above, managed to lower his limp body to the sand.

Will jumped down after him and knelt to untie the rope. "We'll roll him onto one of the blankets and then we can drag him up into the shade of the trees," Will said. It was a hard job. Father lay unmoving and heavy. The sun beat down relentlessly on their unprotected heads. Sweat beaded on Hitty's forehead and dripped down Will's nose. They hauled the blanket, their arms aching. Finally they reached the shelter of the trees and dropped, panting, to the ground.

"Now what should we do?" Hitty asked. "He looks awful. He needs a doctor. Will! I'm scared."

"Well, there isn't a doctor here," Will said. He fished a grubby-looking handkerchief out of his pocket. "First I'm going to clean away all this blood." He ran down to the water's edge, dipped the handkerchief in the ocean, and ran back. Carefully he bathed Father's face, wiping away the dried blood to reveal a deep cut on his forehead.

"See what's in the first-aid kit, Hitty."

The kit was in a white metal box with a red cross painted on the cover. Hitty snapped it open. "Castor oil," she said, wrinkling her nose and making a face. "Why would they put that *in a first-aid kit? Lots of bandages. And iodine. That might help." Cautiously they dabbed the wound with the iodine and wrapped Father's head with strips of gauze bandages.*

Father slowly opened his eyes. "Will?" he said weakly. "Hitty? What happened? Are you all right?"

"We're fine," Will said, "but the plane isn't."

"We crashed into some trees," said Hitty. "The plane's over there."

Father tried to lift his head to look, but dropped quickly back to the sand. His eyes closed again. The children gazed at each other worriedly.

"We have to find help somewhere," Hitty said. "He could die *without medicine. Do you think there are any other people on this island?"*

"We'd better find out," said Will.

CHAPTER 12

The Hidden Hut

Leaving Father carefully covered with the second blanket, the children walked along the sand, peering back into the leafy tangle of trees and vines that bordered the beach.

"We can't get in there," said Hitty. "It's too thick. We'd need a machete."

"Wait a minute," said Will. "Look. Isn't that a trail?"

There was a wide tramped-down swath through the wilderness, as though many stamping feet–"Or some very large animal?" Hitty said nervously–had often passed through.

"It could be people," said Will. "Perhaps it even leads to a village. Let's follow it."

The trail meandered lazily, twisting and turning through trees and underbrush. Hanging vines with dangling watermelon pink flowers swooped down and brushed the children's faces. Bright blue butterflies fluttered past. High above their heads in the trees they saw small green-and-yellow birds–"Parakeets?" asked Will–and tiny iridescent flashes of scarlet and blue, which Hitty thought were hummingbirds. The only sounds were bird songs. There was no sign of human beings.

"We've been gone a long time," Hitty said finally. "Maybe we should turn back. I don't want to leave Father alone for too long."

"The path seems to be getting wider up ahead," said Will. "Maybe there's a village there, or a house. Let's go just a little farther."

They walked on, rounded a gentle curve, and came abruptly to the end of the trail. It stopped at a wide clearing in the underbrush, in the middle of which sat an immense hut, roofed with branches and woven vines. The children stared at it in astonishment. There was no door. The huge hut stood open to the sun and wind. Will and Hitty cautiously tiptoed closer. A sign next to the front step read TRESPASSERS WILL BE PROSECUTED *in elaborate Gothic lettering.*

"Not very friendly, whoever lives here," said Will. "Anyway, no one's home now."

"Who could live here?" wondered Hitty. "It's so strange. Like a Robinson Crusoe house for a giant."

"It's full of wonderful things," said Will, peering curiously inside. "Look, Hitty! There's a giant clamshell!"

A mammoth clamshell, as big as the copper laundry kettle back home, leaned against one wall. Next to it was a grass basket, almost as tall as Hitty herself, which seemed to be full of glistening pearls. A crude wooden table held a collection of beetles carefully labeled and pinned to boards, a terrarium containing an energetic pair of shiny red frogs, a pile of strangely shaped seedpods, a fish skeleton, and a magnifying glass. Against the back wall stood an upright piano with a row of wax candles stuck in colored bottles on top of it. There was a bookcase stuffed with leather-bound books. "The Voyage of the Beagle," *Will read, "by Charles Darwin.* Chesterton's Practical Shipbuilding. Astronomy for Amateurs. The Handbook of Wildflowers. Fossils and How to Find Them." *There was an easel holding a half-finished painting–a seascape with a lot of splashy blue waves– and a bench on which sat a row of large clay pots. Hitty touched one experimentally with her finger. It was still wet.*

"Whoever lives here hasn't been gone for very long," she said.

"Whoever lives here is coming back," said Will. "Listen!"

There was a rustling, shuffling sound, growing louder as it approached the hut. There was a weighty feel to the sound. It seemed to quiver and vibrate through the ground beneath their feet. It was a sound of something threateningly large.

"That doesn't sound like a person," quavered Hitty.

"It isn't!" hissed Will. "Let's get out of here! Let's hide!"

But it was too late. As the children emerged from the hut, its owner rounded the curve of the path and came into view. For one heart-stopping moment, no one moved or breathed. Then Will and Hitty clutched each other, and Hitty burst into tears.

There before them, with an unmistakable expression of annoyance on its face, stood a dragon. Its scales flashed dappled gold in the sunlight filtering through the branches of the trees, and on its back was folded a pair of polished golden wings. Its eyes were a cool silver gray. In its front claws it carried a basket filled with abalone shells. It set the basket down, wiped its claws on the grass in a fussy manner, and gave an impatient snort.

"For heaven's sake, young lady," the dragon said in a snappish tone of voice, "please stop that unsightly snuffling."

Will put a brotherly arm around Hitty's shoulders. "She's scared," he said stoutly. "In all the fairy tales and legends, dragons eat maidens. Are you going to eat us?"

The dragon glared at them scornfully. "Certainly not," it said. It gestured at the sign at the hut entrance. "Trespassers," it announced pointedly, "will be prosecuted. *Not eaten. Dragons are not savages." It tossed its head and muttered angrily to itself. "Really . . ." Hitty and Will heard it saying indistinctly, "no privacy these days. . . . The unbelievable ignorance . . ."*

"Please, sir," Will said apologetically, "we didn't mean to intrude. We were just trying to find help. Our father . . ."

But the dragon had drawn itself up and was looking, if possible, even more peevish than before. "You may address me," it said haughtily, "as ma'am. Sir *is, of course, appropriate for my brothers, but I prefer my proper title."*

"Brothers?" said Will, looking sharply over his shoulders, but Hitty nudged him and pointed. The dragon had three heads. There, almost hidden beneath the folded golden wings, were two more heads, necks coiled low, eyes closed, sound asleep. "I think those must be her brothers," Hitty whispered.

"Precisely, young lady." The dragon nodded. "We are a tridrake. Our name is Fafnyr. Fafnyr Goldenwings."

"I'm Will," said Will, "and this is my sister, Hitty."

"I'm sure I would be very pleased to meet you," said the dragon, "if I had any interest in company. However, I deliberately chose this island for its lack of human beings. I need solitude for my scientific and artistic

pursuits." The dragon glared resentfully at the children, down the full length of its golden nose. "It seems," it said crossly, "that there are no safe places left. You creatures take up an indecent amount of space. You spread across the globe like . . . ," it paused for a moment, searching for a word, "like ants."

"Well, we're not here on purpose," Will said. "We never intended to come here at all. We were on our way around the world by airplane. Our plane crashed on the beach and our father, who was flying it, was injured."

The dragon looked unsympathetic. "And that," it said snootily, "should teach you to stay on the ground, where your kind belongs."

"You don't understand," Hitty cried, her eyes filling again with tears. "Our father is hurt. *And we don't have anywhere to sleep or anything to eat* or anything!"

Without a word, the dragon stalked past the children and entered the hut. Will and Hitty could hear it thumping crossly about inside, opening and closing cupboard doors. Presently it reappeared, holding a small glass bottle. "Give him two of these tablets every four hours," the dragon said, "for fever and pain. As for food and shelter," the dragon looked Hitty and Will coldly up and down, "you look to be strong and competent children. Use your heads."

The dragon vanished indoors. "Good-bye!" it snapped, its back turned. It was clear that the meeting was over.

"Good-bye!" Hitty and Will echoed dismally. Then, holding the little bottle of pills, they retreated back down the trail toward the beach. They continued to peek back curiously as long as the hut was in sight, but the dragon remained invisible. Then, faintly, there came the sound of a piano.

The dragon was playing "A Bicycle Built for Two."

CHAPTER 13

Survivors

Father was awake when the children returned to the beach, but he was burning with fever and barely able to speak above a whisper. Hitty and Will gave him a drink from the water bottle and two of the dragon's little white pills. "I'll be better in the morning,"

Father whispered weakly. "We'll make some plans. . . ."

"It's all right, Father," Will said. "Everything's fine."

"Just rest," said Hitty. "Go to sleep."

As Father slept, the children sipped some of the bottled water, ate crackers, and discussed what to do.

"We need a hut, like the dragon's," Hitty said suddenly and decisively. "And I think I know how to build one. We can prop up some fallen branches like a tepee and hold them together with vines. Did you see the dragon's roof? It was vines, woven in and out. Over and under, just like making potholders on the loom at school."

Will looked at her with new respect. "All right," he said. "Let's collect some branches and vines. I'll help you."

By the time they finished their hut, it was dark and a full moon had risen. The hut was small, but snug, and it felt safe and cozy to be together under a roof—even if they were lost somewhere in the middle of the Pacific Ocean, with no way of getting home. Hitty and Will curled up next to Father on the warm sand, using rolled-up jackets as pillows.

"Crackers again for breakfast," Will murmured sleepily.

"We'll think of something," Hitty whispered back. "Remember what the dragon said. We have to use our heads."

When Will woke the next morning, Hitty was gone. Following her tracks in the soft sand, he found her down at the water's edge, lying on her stomach on some rocks overlooking a deep tidal pool.

"Hitty! I was worried. I didn't know where you were. What are you doing?" asked Will.

"Shh," said Hitty. "I'm fishing." She held a long forked stick in her hand, at the end of which was fastened a small net.

"Where did you get that?" asked Will. He squatted down on the rock next to Hitty and peered hopefully into the water.

"I found the stick on the beach," said Hitty, "and the net is the string bag I had my bathing things in. It makes a wonderful fishing net." Slowly she dipped the net into the pool. Suddenly she made a quick scoop and hoisted the net out of the water. There, thrashing in the string bag, was a fat fish.

"Breakfast!" said Hitty proudly.

They cleaned the fish with Will's pocket-

knife and cooked it on pointed sticks over a fire of driftwood. Father woke up briefly and had a few bites of fish, half a cracker, a drink of water, and two more of the dragon's white pills. Weakly he tried to smile. "Thanks, kids," he said. Then he slept again.

Over the next several days, Will and Hitty learned to live on the island. They found coconuts and cracked them open with pointed rocks, drinking the sweet milk and eating the white meat inside. Hitty went fishing every morning and Will dug clams on the beach, which the children roasted over the coals of their fire. Hitty collected wide flat shells to use as plates and Will used his pocketknife to whittle forks and spoons out of driftwood. They made three sleeping mats for the hut, from layers of soft broad leaves, and each night before bed, they sat outside on the sand, listening to the slow roll of the waves and watching for falling stars. Hitty made them each a hat out of woven palm fronds, to protect them from the sun. They stopped wearing shoes.

When their bottled water ran out, they went exploring once again and found a tiny freshwater stream that, followed back through the trees, led to a miniature sparkling waterfall. A series of deep pits was dug in the stream bank, and there were confused marks of large clawed tracks and a trail of something being dragged. "Look, Hitty," said Will, "this must be where the dragon gets her clay."

Hitty was already scrabbling in the muddy holes. "I'm going to dig some too," she said. "We can make pots and bowls of our own and dry them in the sun."

Each day they hoped for a passing ship–"They must be looking for us by now," Will said–but no one came.

"We can't go on like this," Hitty said finally one morning. "There are thousands of tiny islands in the Pacific. They may never find us. I think we should go ask the dragon for help."

"She doesn't want to see us," said Will. "She doesn't want people around."

"Well, maybe she'll help us just to get us out of her hair," Hitty said.

This time as they rounded the path to the dragon's hut, they heard a voice, reciting. The dragon was home. "'My heart leaps up when I behold,'" she was saying flutily, "'a . . . some-thing *. . . in the sky.' . . . Drat . . . !" There was a hasty rustle of pages. The dragon was memorizing poetry.*

"It's rainbow,*" Hitty whispered loudly to Will. "'My heart leaps up when I behold a* rainbow *in the sky.' William Wordsworth. We had to learn it at school."*

The dragon poked its head out of the hut. It held a red-covered book in one claw. "Ah," it said in unenthusiastic tones. "Visitors."

"We're sorry to disturb you, ma'am," Will said politely.

"We were just wondering," Hitty said, "if you could give us some help."

The dragon closed the book with a snap. "You don't look," it said, "as though you need any. You seem healthy and well fed. Doing quite well for yourselves, I would say. Except, perhaps . . ." The dragon critically surveyed first one child and then the other. "I would suggest more regular baths."

Will looked at his bare feet and Hitty blushed.

"It's not that," Hitty said. "At least, we'll try to. Take baths, I mean. Our real problem is getting off the island. We don't want to stay here forever and I know you don't want us around. And our father needs to see a doctor. Couldn't you help us get back home?"

The dragon snorted and puffed out an

impatient cloud of smoke. “Impossible just now,” it said. “I am in the midst of a series of botanical experiments, studying photosynthesis in seaweeds. Pho-to-syn-the-sis,*” it repeated distinctly, when Hitty and Will looked puzzled, “is the process by which plants convert sunlight into food.”*

“You mean,” said Hitty, her voice rising in dismay, “that you think weeds *are more important than people?”*

The dragon glared at her coldly. “I am afraid,” it said, “that you lack the scientific mind.” It turned and swept briskly back into the hut. Over its shoulder, it spoke one last time. “For heaven’s sake, use your heads,” it said. “Have you tried signaling?*” Then the sound of rustling pages began again.*

“Well,” said Will, “I guess that’s that.”

“Signaling,” Hitty said thoughtfully. “I think I have an idea.”

There were parachutes in the cockpit of the plane. Will watched as Hitty gleefully pulled one from its pouch and spread it out on the sand, an enormous stretch of white-and-orange silk, fastened to a canvas harness. Hitty rocked back on her heels and grinned up at Will.

"We should have thought of this before," she said, gesturing at the opened parachute. "Look at this. It's a perfect signal flag."

"You mean just leave it here on the beach?" Will said. "I don't see what good that will do."

"No." Hitty shook her head. "We're going to fly it. If we get it up to the top of one of those palm trees, the wind will billow it out like a flag. Anyone passing by should be able to see it from miles away. Look how bright it is."

It was awkward climbing with the parachute bundled in her arms, but Hitty managed, clinging to the tree trunk with her free hand and bare feet, like a monkey. At the top of the tree, she wrapped the canvas harness straps tightly around the stubby branches, spread the parachute silk as best she could, and flung it upward into the air. The wind caught it and filled it out, a huge ballooning mushroom of orange and white. Below her on the beach, Will jumped up and down and cheered.

"You did it, Hitty!" he shouted. "A signal flag!"

Hitty dropped down beside him on the sand. "I don't know why we didn't think of it before," she said.

The signal flag flew day and night above the palm tree, snapping and flapping in the ocean breeze. Father was better now, able to sit up for short periods at mealtimes and once even to hobble out onto the beach for a nap in the sun. The children built a small fireplace of flat stones, collected from the shallow water on the north side of the island, and arranged logs around it to serve as benches. They made a rack of branches tied with vines, on which they hung their clothes to dry after washing them in the ocean. Hitty fashioned a set of clay checkers–half marked with the letter H for Hitty, half with a W for Will–and the children played on a board drawn in the sand with a stick.

The days passed slowly, with no sign of rescue. No ship sailed by and no plane flew overhead. "It looks like we're here forever," said Hitty. Will sighed.

Then one afternoon they had an unexpected caller. Father, still weak, was asleep in the hut. Will and Hitty were on the beach, bowling with a pair of coconuts for balls and a set of driftwood chunks for pins, when a great shadow swept across the sand. There was a thunderous sound of beating wings overhead and a scent of spices and smoke. The dragon landed. For a moment it studied their little camp: the hut, the fireplace, the drying rack, the row of clay pots arranged on a log bench, the grass basket filled with fruit, the checkerboard, outlined with pebbles, in the sand. Then it looked up at the parachute waving overhead as a signal flag.

Slowly it gave an approving nod. "Well done," it said to the children. "Very well done. No young dragon could have done better." It looked again toward the hut. "Your father is inside?" it asked. "I should like to meet him."

Father had heard the sound of the dragon's landing. Painfully, leaning on a stick, he limped out of the hut. "Will!" he called. "Hitty! What . . . ?" Then he simply stood still, gaping open-mouthed at the dragon.

The dragon politely inclined its head. "I trust your health is improved, sir?" it inquired.

Father gulped unbelievingly and nodded. "Yes," he said, in a choked voice. "Thank you."

The dragon settled itself on the sand. "Upon reflection," it said, "I find that I have been a bit hasty. Inconsiderate. Even"–the dragon looked down at its feet–"neglectful of duty. It is always important to help those in need." It shuffled its front claws in an embarrassed manner. "Therefore," it said, "I have reconsidered your problem and I have a proposition to make." It curled and uncurled its golden tail. "You would like to return to the mainland. I will take you there. However, there is a condition."

"What condition?" asked Will.

"What do you mean?" asked Hitty.

"As you know," continued the dragon, "I value my privacy. I will not have shiploads of strangers or persons in those . . . ," it paused, looking pointedly at the crumpled wreck of the airplane, "aerial contraptions . . . crashing about on my island, disturbing my peace, and interrupting my experiments." The dragon sighed. "There are so few places left," it said.

"We would never tell anybody," Hitty began, but the dragon held up an admonitory claw.

"We dragons have a talent," it said. "We can cause you to forget."

"You mean like amnesia?" asked Will. "We won't remember where we were or anything that happened?"

"How do you do it?" asked Hitty.

"Just look into my eyes," the dragon said, and turned its cool silver gaze on Hitty. "Just look into my eyes."

As Hitty stared directly into the dragon's eyes, they seemed to grow deeper, wider, cooler, until she was engulfed in a swirl of silver. Her own eyes began to blur, and the world around her swayed softly out of focus, becoming more and more dreamlike and far away with each passing moment. Nothing seemed quite real. . . .

With a jerk of her head, Hitty tore her eyes away. She felt dizzy and disoriented. The beach seemed to waver up and down under her feet.

"You see?" the dragon said. "I can take away all your memories of the island. Of me." It waved a claw at the little camp. "Of all this," it said.

Father cleared his throat. "It's fine with me," he said. "There's nothing here I want to remember. As long as we can all get back home again."

But Hitty ran forward and laid a hand on the dragon's golden scales. "Oh, please, no!" she cried. "Please! I'll never tell! I promise! As long as you'll let me remember you!"

Will stepped forward. "And me," he said.

"I don't want to forget you either. I promise too, Fafnyr."

The dragon looked slowly from Hitty to Will and back again. It studied their upturned faces. Then it nodded its head.

"Now," it said, "please take down that annoying signal flag."

❧ ❧ ❧

They flew by night, sailing dreamlike over endless water. There was a thin crescent of moon and the stars were reflected beneath them, glittering in the dark rolling sea. They hung from the dragon's claws, safely wrapped in a hammock made from the white-and-orange parachute. Father, hypnotized by Fafnyr's cool silver eyes, slept. Hitty and Will were wide awake. Wind rushed warmly through their hair and from above them came the rhythmic comforting thrum of powerfully beating wings.

"We'll be home soon, Hitty," Will said in Hitty's ear. "Home. Doesn't that sound good? Ice-cream sodas and sleeping in your own bed again. . . ."

"And Mother," Hitty said. "She'll have

been so worried. Still . . ." She looked up at the shining golden dragon, winging its way steadily through the summer night. "Still, I hate for this to be over."

Will reached down and squeezed her hand.

Hours later, they landed on another, colder beach. The dragon laid them down gently on the sand. The children crawled out of the entangling folds of parachute and stood up. Above them shone the yellow lights in the windows of a house.

"Our house," said Will. "At last. Thank you for everything, Fafnyr."

"Your father will wake up soon," the dragon said. "I suggest you have a suitable story prepared. Perhaps you were picked up by a passing ship while he was ill."

"We'll think of something," said Will. "We won't give you away. Don't worry."

Hitty laid a hand on the dragon's smooth golden scales.

"Where will you go from here?" she asked. "Back to your hut on the island?"

The dragon was silent for a moment. "I think not, my dear," the dragon said. "Your arrival, from the standpoint of privacy, was the beginning of the end. It is clearly only a *matter of time before others follow in your . . . er . . . footsteps."*

"But if you don't go back . . . ," began Will.

"I must consider," the dragon said. "There are so few places left. Antarctica, perhaps? Still quite empty." Its voice dropped and it seemed to be talking to itself. "But so unpleasantly cold. And all those monotonous penguins."

"Fafnyr," Hitty said suddenly, "you could stay here."

"This is a private island," said Will. "I mean, our family owns it. Nobody lives here but us. We go back and forth to the mainland by boat." He pointed across the dark water to the distant lights of a town.

"At the north end of the island," said Hitty, "there's a hill, and in it there's a cave. Nobody ever goes there. We went inside it just once, with a lantern. It's enormous. You'd be safe living there forever. And we'd never tell anyone about you–never, as long as we live."

The dragon's silver eyes glistened, and its voice, for a moment, wavered.

"A Resting Place," it said. It looked from Hitty to Will and back again. "I am staggered," the dragon said. "I am overwhelmed."

"A Resting Place?" asked Will.

"A Resting Place," the dragon said, "is a sanctuary. An utterly safe and hidden place. A haven." Then it said, in more down-to-earth tones, "A good place to sleep."

"You'll be quite alone there," said Hitty. "It's very peaceful."

"I am in your debt," the dragon said. "I accept your most generous offer." It blinked rapidly and sniffed. "Perhaps you would come and visit me sometimes."

Then the dragon said solemnly, "Please hold out your hands."

Hitty and Will, exchanging a puzzled glance, each held out a hand, palm upward. The dragon lifted a golden claw and pricked their extended hands, precisely in the center. Hitty gave a little cry of surprise. There was a sharp sting, which quickly vanished, followed by a soothing warmth. The children stared, wide-eyed, at their hands.

"I sparkle," said Hitty, in a whisper.

Will said, "So do I."

In the center of each child's hand was a tiny gleaming point of dragon-gold.

"We are bonded," said the dragon huskily.

"I am sorry I misjudged you in the early days of our acquaintance. You are true Dragon Friends."

There was a heartfelt pause.

"The gift of your cave," the dragon said. "That was a dragonish thing to do."

"We'll never forget what you did for us, Fafnyr," Hitty said. "We wouldn't have survived without you."

The great golden dragon bent down and gently smoothed the hair of first one, then the other, with a polished claw. "Ah, yes, you would, my dear," the dragon said. It tapped Hitty lightly on the forehead. "Use your head," it said. "It was all right there, all the time."

Then with a pounding rush of wings, the dragon rose into the air and turned toward the north. Hitty and Will stood looking after it, until it had faded in the distance, into an almost invisible pinprick of gold."

Chapter 14

Farewell

"And is that the end of the story?" asked Hannah.

"It can't be," said Zachary. "What happened to Will? Did he become a pilot when he grew up?"

The dragon bristled. "Certainly not," it said. "He had more sense. He became a famous botanist, a world expert on marine plants. A new species of seaweed was named after him, but he always preferred its common name. He called it dragonweed."

"What about Hitty?" asked Sarah Emily. "She was my favorite. What happened to her?"

The dragon inclined its golden head. "Why," it said, "I thought you knew. For heaven's sake, child, use your head!"

Sarah Emily thought for a moment and suddenly her eyes opened wide. "Hitty!" she said. "It's a nickname for Mehitabel. Hitty is Aunt Mehitabel!"

"It was Aunt Mehitabel who told us to explore

Drake's Hill," Hannah said. "She must have wanted us to find you here."

The dragon bent its head. "She is an honored and beloved friend," it said, "and very wise. She has kept the Resting Place safe for many years."

"She sends you her regards," Sarah Emily said softly.

"I miss her visits," the dragon said.

"She's very old now," Hannah said gently. "She has to walk with a stick. I know she would come if she could."

"We'll keep the Resting Place safe, too, Fafnyr," said Zachary. "We'll never tell anyone either."

"We all promise," said Hannah.

"And if you ever need any help . . . ," began Sarah Emily.

The dragon nodded. "Thank you, my dears," it said. Then it said, "Please hold out your hands."

The three children each held out a hand, the palm facing upward. Slowly and ceremoniously the dragon extended a golden claw. It pricked each outstretched hand, precisely in the center; first Hannah's, then Zachary's, and finally Sarah Emily's. Each child felt a sharp stinging pain, then a beautiful feeling of well-being and warmth. Sarah Emily raised her hand toward her face.

"It *does* sparkle," she breathed.

"We are bonded," the great golden dragon said.

"Oh, Fafnyr," Hannah said shakily. "We are honored."

Zachary reverently touched the tiny golden glitter in the center of his palm. Then he looked up, regretfully. "It's getting late," he said. "We should go before people start wondering where we are. Thank you, Fafnyr, for everything."

"And thank your brothers for us," added Hannah.

The dragon nodded. The golden head drooped. The silver eyes closed. The light in the cave grew dim. Softly the children turned to leave.

Sarah Emily lingered behind.

"Will we see you again, Fafnyr?" she asked. "We don't live here, you know. We're just visiting and we'll have to go home soon. It could be a whole year before . . ."

She stopped. The dragon was asleep.

Sadly Sarah Emily turned to follow Zachary and Hannah. She groped her way carefully upward, running one hand along the rocky wall. Then a husky voice spoke behind her out of the darkness.

"When you come back," the dragon said, "we will still be here."

A letter arrived at last from Aunt Mehitabel, sweepingly addressed to the children in peacock blue ink. "By now," wrote Aunt Mehitabel, "you know the secret of Drake's Hill. The time has come for me to pass on the trust. I am not getting any younger and Fafnyr needs friends and protectors. I feel sure that you three will keep the Resting Place safe."

"But why didn't she just tell us about Fafnyr?" Sarah Emily asked.

Hannah smiled over the top of the letter. "There's a P.S. at the end," she said, "and it's underlined in gold ink. It says, 'Some things are best when you discover them for yourself.'"

Zachary chuckled. "She sounds just like Fafnyr," he said.

Sarah Emily said, "She sounds like Hitty."

The time had come to leave the island. Suitcases and duffle bags were packed. Shell collections were carefully wrapped in newspaper. Bathrooms and bedside tables were checked for things left behind. The children hugged Mrs. Jones, who hugged each of them tight and pressed bags of fresh oatmeal cookies into their hands. "You'll be back next summer," she said, "and it will be here sooner than you think, so don't let me see any of those long faces. You watch: It will be June quicker than a wink, and you'll all be here to help me make strawberry jam and blueberry pies."

"And dig clams," put in Mr. Jones, "and keep a weather eye on the night sky." He patted Zachary on the shoulder. "The captain's telescope will be here waiting for you, young man."

The children looked mournfully around the house one last time.

"I hate leaving," Sarah Emily said. "I wish we could stay here forever."

"I'll miss everything about this place," said Hannah. "Even that awful elephant's-foot stool."

"But what we'll all miss most . . . ," began Zachary. Then he stopped abruptly and turned away to look out the window.

"Fafnyr," Sarah Emily whispered.

"Fafnyr," said Hannah. There was a catch in her voice.

They trooped sadly down to the shore and loaded their belongings onto the now-familiar green boat, the *Martha*. Mother tucked the last bag under the seat in the bow. "Just one more look around," she said, straightening up. "It's been a wonderful summer. And it's been good for you children, spending time here. We'll come back again."

There was a sound of boots crunching over sand and stones as Mr. Jones approached. "All aboard," he said. They climbed reluctantly into the boat. Sarah Emily cast off and the *Martha* chugged westward toward the mainland and home. The island began to grow smaller and smaller in the distance. The children sat up straighter, gazing longingly back at it over the swelling blue waves.

"Good-bye, Fafnyr," whispered Zachary.

"Good-bye, Fafnyr," murmured Hannah. Her eyes were filled with tears.

But Sarah Emily looked straight into the wind, with a look of pride and determination on her face. "We'll always remember!" she shouted as loudly as she could. "And we'll be back!"

In the far distance behind them, from the receding peak of Drake's Hill, came—for just an instant—a dazzling sunbeam flash of pure gold.